The Bronxville Book Club

The Bronxville Book Club

Pamela Hackett Hobson

iUniverse, Inc.
New York Lincoln Shanghai

The Bronxville Book Club

iUniverse, Inc.

For information address:
iUniverse
2021 Pine Lake Road, Suite 100
Lincoln, NE 68512
www.iuniverse.com

The Bronxville Book Club is a work of fiction. Names, characters, places and incidents either are the product of the author's imagination or are used fictitiously.

ISBN: 0-595-28351-9 (Pbk)
ISBN: 0-595-65767-2 (Cloth)

Printed in the United States of America

For Bob, Tom and Mike

You are the wind beneath my wings.

~

Acknowledgments

I owe a million thanks to Patty, Peggy, Bob, and Allison who supported the book from the very first outline through multiple drafts. I also want to thank the "font-anstic" Tom, and his wonderful Photography Assistant, Michael, for contributing their exceptional talents to the creation of the novel's cover. I could not have written this book without the many suggestions and words of encouragement from all throughout the entire process.

A big thank you to Dad, and my entire family, for your unwavering support, love and continued belief in me.

Thank you to the women in my own "Bronxville Book Clubs" with whom I have had the pleasure of sharing books and friendship. A special thanks to Ann, whose spectacular library provided incredible inspiration, and whose honest feedback on the very first draft was much appreciated.

Thank you, Boba, my unparalleled (and unpaid) agent.

And last but not least, thank you, Mom. I know you would have been proud.

The Bronxville Book Club

"True friends stab you in the front."

Oscar Wilde

Table of Contents

Prologue

Prologue

The Bronxville Book Club

****

To: *brokerbabe@bxvillerealestate.com,*
munnyhunny@jaegerwood.com,
legalgenius@carruthersassoc.com,
greenthum@graciousgardens.com,
horsewhisperer@equestriansociety.org,
arichardson@annetiques.com,
bronxvillegrad@nyjuniorleague.com,
christmascarole@eventplanning.org,
modelcitizen@thelingerielady.com,
pcdoc@systemsolutions.com,
maestramama@westchesterteachers.edu,
bookworm@literaryreview.com,
inhumanresource@womeninbanking.com,
never2thin@fitness.org

From: *whippenpoof@thebronxvillebookclub.com*

Subject: *The Bronxville Book Club Meeting*

Date: *May 15*

Time: *7:30 p.m.*

Place: *Kathryn Chasen's home*
101 Masterton Road
Bronxville, New York

Book: *I Don't Know How She Does It: The Life of Kate*
Reddy, Working Mother by Allison Pearson

Hope to see you all there!

****

"*Do not employ handsome servants.*"

Chinese Proverb

Chapter 1

Kathryn

brokerbabe@bxvillerealestate.com

athryn was out of time. A quick glance at her diamond-studded Rolex, a wedding gift from David, confirmed what she already knew. It was 5:26, and in two short hours her book club members would begin pulling into the circular driveway of her home on Masterton Road. With all that had happened today, it was just her luck that tonight it was her turn to host the monthly meeting.

This had not been one of Kathryn's better days since joining Bronxville Real Estate Partners. The closing scheduled for tomorrow was in jeopardy…the ad for Sunday's Open House was overdue…and she'd just discovered that Houlihan Lawrence had snagged the listing for the $3.24 million Bowman mansion on the Hilltop. Still reeling from that bit of news, Kathryn retrieved one missed message from her cell phone. "Hi, Mrs. Chasen, it's Leslie. I am so sorry, but I have tons of homework and can't sit for Pryce tonight." Unfortunately, Pryce also had a lot of homework that needed to be supervised, and now Kathryn would have to squeeze that in before her guests arrived. Fourth grade math and all the preparation for state tests were turning out to be more difficult and stressful than Kathryn could have imagined. For that matter, Kathryn's whole life was turning out to be more difficult and stressful than she ever could have imagined.

It wasn't always like this. Kathryn could clearly remember the surprise trip to Paris where P. David Chasen III proposed over dinner at *L'Orangerie* and presented her with a 3-carat Tiffany diamond ring. Immediately upon their return to New York, Kathryn spent every waking minute planning a wedding fit for a royal couple. Her dear friend Willis, who owned *Kensington Paper*, designed the pearl-white invitations and personally oversaw the engraving of each one. Kathryn's Vera Wang gown, a silk-organza, strapless ball gown, featuring a French hand-beaded bodice, looked exquisite on her tall, slim frame. The elaborately-jeweled tiara sat perfectly atop her elegant blonde chignon. On a picture-perfect June day, Kathryn's father offered his arm and walked his beautiful daughter down the aisle at the Reformed Church. In a moving ceremony presided over by Reverend Steele, Kathryn and David, surrounded by two hundred-fifty of their closest friends, family members, and business associates, said, "I do." Immediately after the ceremony, a Rolls Royce whisked the newlyweds off to a dinner reception at *The Pierre*. Dancing to the music of a fifteen-piece orchestra went on well into the night, long after the wedding cake with layers of white fondant icing covered in pastel-colored flowers was served.

Returning from a spectacular honeymoon in Tuscany, the happy couple settled into their seven-bedroom Tudor home on Masterton Road in Bronxville. Kathryn understood completely why Bronxville was known as the Village "that is endlessly copied but never matched." Located in southern Westchester County, Bronxville had a well-earned reputation as a charming English-style village only 18 miles from Manhattan. With such proximity, David's driver could deliver him to his midtown office in less than 20 minutes.

Depending on the season, the couple spent their weekends golfing at the Siwanoy Country Club, sailing at their summer home in Southampton, skiing at their lodge in Vail, or hosting theatre parties at their upper East Side penthouse. With Kathryn's eagerly anticipated pregnancy, Anjolie was added to the ever-expanding household staff as Head Nanny to prepare for the newest member of the Chasen family. Anjolie, who had attained highest honors on the Nanny Credential Exam, quickly assimilated into her new surroundings. Surrounded by such support, Kathryn sailed through the final months of her pregnancy enjoying the well deserved "perks" of her marriage to David. She hardly minded that as time went by, David was spending more time in the city due to last-minute crises at his investment management firm. After all, she and Pryce needed to be kept in the manner to which she had become accustomed. David encouraged Kathryn to continue to enjoy her weekends away while the highly capable Anjolie tended the home fires.

Unfortunately, Anjolie was tending more than the home fires. By the time Kathryn was enlightened by a well-meaning "friend" in town, it was over. The homes, the cars, the portfolio, the club memberships, and of course, the friends, were quickly divvied up. Although Kathryn managed to hold on to the Bronxville estate and the condo in Vail, the alimony was just not covering all of her expenses. Was it really possible that her taxes were now more than the average salary of a schoolteacher in Manhattan?

Thank God Kathryn's father had insisted years ago that she sit for her realtor license, since he thought it would give her something to do until she met Mr. Right. Was it only one year ago that Kathryn had enjoyed visiting the homes of David's friends, and conversationally sharing her expert advice on which home improvements would significantly increase the resale value of their properties? Now Kathryn was desperately aware that if she didn't close at least four listings before year-end, she would be in serious financial straits. And those four sales needed to be on properties located in the village of Bronxville—not Bronxville vicinity, Bronxville Border, Bronxville Manor, or Bronxville Post Office—in order to generate the hefty commissions Kathryn needed to keep afloat.

To further complicate matters, as a fourth-grader in the Bronxville Elementary School, Pryce was becoming a handful. Kathryn wanted to be around more, but her clients always seemed to need their hands held at just the moment that he needed her time and attention. With a live-in nanny now a luxury she simply could not afford, Kathryn depended on the Sarah Lawrence and Concordia college students to cover after school, evenings and weekends. That worked fine, unless five minutes before they were due to arrive, something just happened to come up. Like tonight.

Kathryn needed to focus. Her number one priority was getting the ad for Sunday's Open Houses to Marina, her contact at the *New York Times*, before Marina left for the day. While scribbling some last minute changes to the copy, Kathryn dialed Marina's number.

****

WELCOME HOME!

Expansive porch welcomes you to this 7 bdrm, 5 and one-half bath Classic Colonial. Bedroom and living room fireplaces, lg formal DR, huge sunroom & newly renovated kitchen. Exquisite details throughout, including French doors everywhere. Separate au-pair suite with own entrance and bath. Beautifully landscaped private garden.

Bronxville Village #10177
$2,158,500

Open House
Sunday
1:00–3:00 p.m.
Dir. Midland Avenue to
1020 Avon Road

****

WALK TO ALL

Village townhouse in the heart of Bronxville. Move-in condition! 4 bedrooms; 2 and one-half baths; living room with stone fireplace, modern kitchen, cozy breakfast nook. Enjoy the peals of nearby church bells while reading in your English garden.

Bronxville Village #10629
$895,000

Open House
Sunday
1:00–3:00
Dir. Pondfield Road West to
725 Alden Place

Bronxville Real Estate Partners
www.bxvillerealestate.com

****

Marina agreed that if Kathryn e-mailed the ad *immediately*, she would make sure that it got into the Sunday edition. Kathryn pressed her luck and asked if Marina would accept a faxed, handwritten copy instead. Kathryn could barely type at all, never mind quickly. In her wildest dreams, she had never imagined she would need to use her impeccably manicured fingers to do anything more than showcase the latest diamond rings she had been given. After a pregnant pause, Marina relented. The fax would be fine.

With the ad taken care of, Kathryn turned her attention to tomorrow's closing. Her long-time partner, Joan, agreed to keep calling both the buyer and seller's attorneys so that Friday's closing date could still be salvaged. Another postponement meant another delay in Kathryn's commission, and that was not something she wanted to contemplate. With assurances and a friendly push from Joan, Kathryn locked her desk and headed to her car.

Her car. A new, drop-dead gorgeous Mercedes SL500 Roadster in ice blue. The salesman certainly saw her coming. So what if she didn't have David to pay the bills? She was determined to buy herself something ultra luxurious, and this surely fit the bill. After all, she needed to drive her clients around in style. She couldn't be seen taking prospects around in a Taurus, could she? So what if the sticker price was $88,010? Kathryn was confident she could easily sell several showplace homes to cover the payments. Her mind made up, Kathryn's only question for the well-groomed Mercedes salesman was, "How soon can you deliver the car to my door?"

As beautiful as the car was, right now Kathryn was more interested in how quickly it could get her out of the Kensington Road parking lot and over to Pondfield Road. If she didn't get to the *Wine & Spirit Emporium* before it closed, there would be no Chardonnay for her guests. The book club could do without many things, including having read the book, but wine was definitely not one of them.

Securing a coveted parking space next to the wine store, Kathryn reflexively reached for a quarter before remembering it was 6:05, and she needn't feed the meter. As she and any visitor to Bronxville quickly learned, "Meters Enforced" was a sign not to be taken lightly, and she could not afford even one more ticket. Not surprisingly, at the last Village Board

Meeting, Bill Murphy had proudly informed Mayor Hand that permit fees and parking revenues were dramatically ahead of budget. Since moving into Bronxville, Kathryn had contributed more than her fair share to that line item in the budget, which was used to offset some of the costs of maintaining such a high level of village services. After the divorce, Kathryn resolved not to make any more "contributions" to that worthy cause.

Kathryn couldn't remember how late the *Wine & Spirit Emporium* stayed open, but when she saw that there were still customers inside the store, she breathed a sigh of relief. Quickly selecting a case of Kendall Jackson, she charged the $119.88 and loaded it into the car in record time. If she hurried, she could get to the *Food Emporium* to buy some ready-made hors d'ouevres, and still get home in time to tidy up, change, and have a quick bite with Pryce while checking his homework.

There was not enough time for Kathryn to stop in at *Try & Buy* to pick up a "surprise" so that Pryce would agree to stay in his room for the entire meeting. Maybe Kathryn would promise to take him for pizza at *Il Bacio*, followed by a trip to *Candyland*, on Saturday. It was getting harder and harder to compete with the presents David bought him anyway. Kathryn decided it would also be a good idea if she set up the Playstation in Pryce's room so he could keep himself occupied while the women discussed the book.

As stressed as she was, Kathryn really was looking forward to seeing everyone from the book club. Not only did Kathryn enjoy the adult company, but also she relished the opportunity to catch up on the latest news in town. Some prime piece of gossip, such as an imminent divorce or unplanned relocation, might even lead to an exclusive listing. What self-respecting real estate agent could turn down that kind of opportunity? Certainly not one who desperately needed to retain her standing in the Million Dollar Sales Club.

Although there were officially 15 members in the book club, Kathryn expected that fewer than a dozen of the women would actually show up. While that was a manageable group to host, the only potential downside was you never knew exactly which of the members would be able to make it. Although generally a very collegial group, she knew from first hand experience how easily the tenor of the meeting could change depending on the mix of members present.

She just hoped that Lizbet and Anne didn't both show up tonight. If they did, things could get a bit uncomfortable. Lizbet's college roommate lived on Prescott Avenue, right near the site of the "McMansion" Anne was renovating. Lizbet would not be at all interested in listening to Anne's complaints about how unreasonable her neighbors were being over the whole situation. Yet the more Kathryn thought about it, the more she realized she didn't have anything to worry about. Lizbet would never do anything that even remotely involved a breach of good decorum.

Rather than fretting over which book club members would show up, Kathryn knew she should be more concerned about whether Doreena, her new cleaning woman, had shown up this afternoon as promised. Doreena was not the most reliable cleaning woman Kathryn had ever had, but her hourly rate was affordable, and at this point, that was paramount. Parting with her loyal and beloved housekeeper, Mrs. Crawford, had in some ways been more difficult for Kathryn than parting with David.

Mrs. Crawford at least had been faithful.

"*Some people are born on third base and go through life thinking they hit a triple.*"

Barry Switzer

Chapter 2

Lizbet

whippenpoof@thebronxvillebookclub.com

*L*izbet Wellington Smith was feeling terrific. Memorial Day was less than two weeks away, and this year the buzz was incredible. As the main fundraiser for the Bronxville School, the Memorial Day activities were responsible for adding at least $150,000 to the PTA coffers. Lizbet was confident that this year would break all records.

The Games Committee had put together an absolutely amazing program. They would, of course, bring back the old favorites—the Jumping Castle and Dunk Tank—but they also had lined up several new attractions, including a rock-climbing wall and batting cages, which were bound to be hits. More of the students were getting involved, too. The sophomores were setting up a sand-art table, and the juniors were planning a basketball jump shot contest. (Thank goodness for the community service section on the college applications.) Even the traditional events like the *Run for Fun* would get a new twist, with a special division for the "over 50" villagers.

Not to be outdone, the Festival-on-the-Green Committee had also organized a full program of events. The Art Show was coming back, with more local artists contributing their works. After all, Bronxville began as an artist's colony over one hundred years ago. The book sale promised to be its usual success—all the latest hardcover best sellers could be had for only $5.00 each. The Food Court was offering an expanded gourmet menu to supplement the Japanese lunch and traditional barbecue fare. The High School honors jazz band had agreed to play throughout the afternoon. And after such a full day, parents and children could set out their blankets and picnic on the lawn while listening to an oldies band.

Of course, the much-anticipated Silent Auction would continue throughout the weekend. This year Lizbet knew that her committee members had done an outstanding job. They had cajoled, wheedled, begged, bribed, and "guilted" other parents, village residents, and local merchants to donate many valuable items. Even if some of the donations were motivated by keeping up with, well, maybe not the Jones, but certainly the Van der Kellens, who could complain as long as the school benefited? Lizbet remembered the year two fathers got into a frenzied bidding war over tickets to the World Series. Money was definitely no object, which was exactly what Lizbet was counting on.

This year you could bid on a week at a villa in Italy, a condominium in Palm Beach, a ski lodge in Vail (thank you, Kathryn!), or a cabin in the Berkshires. You could add your name to the list for sky box seats at every major sporting event, sailing trips, catered dinners, interior design advice, house seats to Broadway shows, a luncheon at *Tiffany's* (chauffeured limo included), and so on, and so on. Lizbet herself had offered to take a group of eight to a day of beauty at the *Red Door Salon* in Manhattan. Her husband Grant had strong-armed his college roommate into putting together a private tour of the NBC Studios with a one-on-one interview with *Today Show* hosts Katie Couric and Matt Lauer—all for a minimum bid of only $850. Hard to believe, but one of the newest items expected to hit at least four figures in the bidding was a reserved spot in the school parking lot for after-school pickup.

Even with all this activity, Lizbet of course had read the book for tonight's meeting. She couldn't recall who had picked this month's selection, *I Don't Know How She Does It: The Life of Kate Reddy, Working Mother*. Lizbet would have preferred they read a book about mothers like herself, the unsung heroes who tirelessly devoted all their time, talents, and energy to managing and actively participating in their children's academic and social lives. Everyone talked about how busy they were, but surely they could find a few uninterrupted hours to read the book and prepare for the meeting. No one was busier than she was.

In addition to her many volunteer activities, Lizbet was absolutely overwhelmed trying to get Whitney ready for the college admissions game. Of course if she and Grant had their way, Whitney would follow in their footsteps and head off to Yale. But Whitney had some misguided notion that an Ivy League school was not where she wanted to go. Whitney wanted to go to Boston University. BU was a very fine school, but...

Had Lizbet and Grant not devoted the last eighteen years to getting their only child into Yale? Lizbet actually felt it was more like nineteen years, since she counted the year before Whitney was born. If Lizbet and Grant hadn't pulled all those strings to get their unborn daughter a place on waiting list for the 92nd Street Y, the elite preschool in Manhattan, Whitney's future certainly would have been in jeopardy. Lizbet had made sure that Whitney had every possible advantage—private tutors, summer courses in Paris, internships at such distinguished institutions as the *Museum of Modern Art* and *Lincoln Center*. As supportive parents, they also had encouraged Whitney to participate in a multitude of extracurricular activities that were absolutely essential if she was going to have a fighting chance of getting into the Smith's ivy alma mater.

Legacy or not, times had changed and Whitney would need a killer application. True, her accomplishments were many—Captain of the Varsity Field Hockey team, Student Council President, Manager of the Art Fair, Stage Director of the winter play, First Flautist in the Honors Orchestra, and National Merit finalist—but Lizbet still wasn't sure that Whitney had really done enough. Grant had told Lizbet that the consultant they had just hired for $4,000 had better ensure that Whitney's college essay was nothing less than spectacular.

Lizbet was encouraged by the *Worth Magazine* study that noted that those who attended Bronxville High School had better odds of getting into an Ivy League school. Bronxville, in the esteemed company of Spence, Winsor, Phillips Exeter Academy, and Hackley, was one of only six public high schools that made it into the top 100 on this prestigious list. Perhaps at the meeting tonight she would feel out some of the other members who might have a connection on the Admissions Committee at Yale. They knew Whitney and would surely want to help her. Of course, she had to be careful not to discuss Whitney's application to Yale in front of Madison. Lizbet had heard that Madison's son, Cole, also was applying early decision to Yale.

The Smith's housekeeper, Mrs. McGrath, who had made the move with them from New York City, was preparing dinner for the family in the recently renovated country kitchen. The aroma from the scones Mrs. McGrath had baked for Lizbet to bring to the meeting was a reminder to head upstairs and get ready. Lizbet prided herself on being prompt, so she entered the private dressing area off the master bedroom suite and closed the door.

Seated at her Queen Anne cherry vanity table, Lizbet carefully fingered her ash-blonde hair, styled this afternoon at the Neiman salon in the Westchester Mall. Lizbet leaned in closer to the oval mirror to examine her wide-set, turquoise eyes. Dr. Rothman was right—the Botox injections made such a difference. Lizbet picked up a mascara wand in her freshly-manicured right hand and touched up her long lashes. Turning her head side-to-side, Lizbet was satisfied that her face and hair looked just right.

Rising from the dainty vanity bench upholstered in cream damask, Lizbet opened the door to "Her" walk in closet—"His" was just a bit smaller—and perused the racks. She couldn't decide which blouse to wear with her ecru silk-cropped pants—the Tea Rose Heather silk shell, or the Deep Eggplant mock turtleneck with the cap sleeves. She settled on the turtleneck since it went beautifully with the new strappy sandals she'd found at *Plaza Too* last weekend. To complete the outfit, she selected an ecru cashmere sweater to drape over her shoulders and tie loosely around her neck. A splash of Joy Eau de Parfum, and Lizbet was set.

Admiring her reflection in the full-length Cheval mirror, Lizbet was pleased. Thank goodness she spent every other morning playing tennis at the Field Club with Olivia. Maintaining a size six, once effortless, now required a bit more work. But luckily she had inherited her mother's good genes, which she appeared to have passed on to her own daughter. When her personal trainer, Bjorn, came to the house last Wednesday, he told her couldn't believe how much she and Whitney looked like sisters.

As Lizbet turned to check that everything looked perfect whether she was coming or going, Whitney knocked softly on her door. "Mom, can you drop me off at Taylor's house on the way to your book club meeting?" Whitney and Taylor needed to start planning ideas for the senior yearbook, since they were both applying for the coveted Yearbook Editor position. Lizbet was delighted. "Of course, darling. Let's just have a quick bite of Mrs. McGrath's supper first and talk about your strategy. You absolutely must get that job, sweetest."

Lizbet pulled the chain to turn off the Tiffany lamp on her bedside table and thought to herself, "Yearbook Editor...that will look great on Whitney's Yale application."

"*Ask about your neighbors,*
then buy the house."

Jewish Proverb

Chapter 3

Anne

arichardson@annetiques.com

The new boutique on Park Place in Bronxville was all set to go. The Scarsdale and Larchmont venues were practically running themselves, so Anne could afford to devote most of her energies to this new endeavor. After extensive market research, she knew that the Bronxville location would be the jewel in the crown of her very successful antiques business. She sensed that her clientele would be every bit as sophisticated and knowledgeable as the women she consulted with in her other southern Westchester communities. Style, good taste, and an expansive budget—a true recipe for success.

Getting to this point, though, had been very hard work. Donald was not happy about the exorbitant start-up costs for *Annetiques*, but they were unavoidable if one wanted to be successful in such an upscale community. As he of all people knew, if you wanted to make money, you needed to spend money, lots and lots of it. As far as Anne was concerned, she and Donald had a perfect financial arrangement—he made the money, she spent it! The boutique space needed quite a bit of work to bring it up to Anne's exacting standards. She was paying top dollar to hire the best artists to restore the ceiling to its original brilliance with hand-painted frescoes. She had also brought in highly specialized European craftsmen to rewire and retrofit the four individually designed chandeliers they had imported from Austria. As far as the three antique display cabinets they were lucky enough to find and have shipped back from their trip to Spain, Donald didn't expect her to refinish them, did he? And he could hardly quibble about the merchandising consultant she had retained. That woman was well worth her fee many times over—the specialized sales "zones" she created would showcase Anne's favorite, and most expensive, one-of-a-kind collections. With her uncanny eye for exceptional pieces that would match the sensibilities of her clients, Anne knew that this investment would pay for itself many times over.

Although her business was poised to take off, Anne was not enjoying nearly as much success in her personal life and knew she needed advice. The home she and Donald were renovating on Prescott Avenue was creating quite a controversy. She had no idea how much resistance there would be to her very tasteful redesign of the structure that had originally been built in the 1920's. Did her neighbors really expect that three people could live in the home as William Stanley Bates originally designed it?

In her opinion, the house was an old grande dame that had long outlived her prime, desperately crying out to be rebuilt in the much more majestic manner of Anne's childhood home in Atlanta. If one was going to commit the not inconsiderable resources required for such a major undertaking, it stood to reason that one would design a much finer home that took advantage of every inch of the property. Who could possibly find fault with that?

Well, just about everyone had found fault with just about every aspect of her plan. They had even coined a new name for her precious home— *McMansion*. Her neighbors on the left, the Cliffords, had lived in the village for over 40 years, and now they were not even on speaking terms with Anne and Donald Richardson. For that matter, their neighbor on the right, Amy van Dusenberry, wasn't exactly speaking to them either. True, Donald and Anne had removed some of the larger, older trees that bordered Mrs. van Dusenberry's property so that the architect could reclaim the space for an expanded family room and library. However, these improvements were sure to enhance the value not only of the Richardson's home, but also the value of all the homes in the entire neighborhood. If they would only be patient, the Cliffords, Mrs. van Dusenberry, and all of the others in the surrounding homes would grow equally fond of the new trees Anne and Donald would plant to replace those old oaks. Anne would hire the best professional landscaper in Westchester—someone like Chelsea, whom Anne had met through the book club.

Feeling increasingly frustrated, Anne thought it was high time the residents on Prescott saw things from Anne's perspective for a change. If she and Donald didn't add a new third floor, they would not be able to include the absolutely essential two-bedroom guest suite with separate baths, and an art/music studio for their first-grade daughter. Paige, as everyone who met her could immediately tell, was extremely gifted and needed an appropriate space for her budding artistic talents to flourish. The fabulous architect they had hired had even been able to create an additional 24 x 24 foot room off the studio to display Paige's extensive collection of Victorian dollhouses, antique bisque and china dolls, and Steiff Teddy Bears.

Anne knew she was not alone in her desire to improve her property. If her neighbors drove down any street in Bronxville, they would observe the ever-present dumpsters outside so many houses that were undergoing extensive facelifts. The dimensions and original footprints of these homes couldn't possibly suit today's families. The lots on which they were located were just not big enough for today's lifestyles—in a village of one square mile, every inch of space had to be maximized. In fact, her neighbors should be downright grateful to her and Donald for changing the character of the original dwelling. The new home they had commissioned would be far superior.

Perhaps her fellow book club members could help her understand what all the fuss was about. Two months ago, Donald's fraternity brother Kip had introduced Anne to Madison, the wife of his partner's brother. At Anne's urging, Kip had prevailed upon Madison, one of the founding members of the Bronxville Book Club, to secure an invitation for Anne to join the group so she could meet other women in the village. Her girlfriends back home could not believe how many activities in the village required someone's official or unofficial "permission" to join. Rumor had it that the Bronxville Women's Club had denied even Rose Fitzgerald Kennedy membership. Of course, that was back in the 1930's, when Rose and her husband Joe had lived in the town. Something like that would never happen today!

This book club was made up of a diverse group—some were working mothers; others, high-powered women who opted for early "retirement"; and still others who had never worked outside the home. Maybe some of them could help Anne navigate the intricate Zoning Board of Appeals process. She just didn't get it. Perhaps one of them could help her understand what all the "noise" was about. Better yet, perhaps one of the book club members had an "in" on the Zoning Board.

Anne suddenly remembered that Kathryn had mentioned to her that Lizbet's college roommate or sorority sister—Emma Stanford?—lived on Prescott Avenue! What a great opportunity. Tonight Anne would try to pull Lizbet aside at the meeting and enlist her support. Lizbet obviously had impeccable taste—once she understood Anne and Donald's vision for their home and the neighborhood more clearly, surely she would want to help convince her fellow Whippenpoof, Emma, to cease her efforts to block the renovation. Anne and Donald should host an intimate party at the Club and invite both Emma and Lizbet, and their husbands, as their guests. Why hadn't Anne thought of that before?

Anne checked the lapel watch she had picked up at an estate sale in Bedford—7:25 p.m. She had better get moving if she didn't want to be too late for the meeting. Anne rummaged in her purse and found the antique silver compact Donald had given her for their anniversary. Flipping it open, Anne checked her makeup in the beveled mirror—at least all she needed was a quick reapplication of her Lancôme Champagne LipColour. She ran a comb through her honey-blonde, chin-length bob while calling down the hall to her husband.

"Donald, can you please drop me at Kathryn's house on your way over to Prescott Avenue?"

Anne also called for her daughter. "Paige, come give me a kiss goodbye." As Paige bounded into the room, Anne cautioned, "Careful, honey, you don't want to mess up mommy's makeup, do you?"

"Food is an important part of a balanced diet."

Fran Lebowitz

Chapter 4

Hillary

never2thin@fitness.org

*H*illary was still down at the school track. It was just starting to get a bit dark, but she needed to run four more laps before she could head home to do some baking for the book club meeting. If she completed that mile, she wouldn't have to worry about the extra calories from the apple she had eaten at 3:00.

Hillary knew she had to be careful or her weight could balloon up to 95 pounds before she knew it. Now that she was in her early forties, she had to work *extra* hard to maintain her perfect weight of 87 pounds on her 5' 3½" frame. She couldn't bear to see any number beginning with "9" on her bathroom scale. She would not be that fat if it killed her!

She was glad to have the meeting to look forward to tonight. Today had been a particularly aggravating day. Lawrence Hospital was especially busy this time of year, and as the Administrative Manager of the Physical Therapy unit, Hillary was swamped with paperwork and messages to return. When Dr. Westland stopped by earlier and asked her if she had a minute, Hillary had demurred, "No, I really don't have the time now; there is so much going on in PT that I have to take care of personally. If you don't mind, Jim, perhaps we can schedule something for next week?" Jim Westland very kindly, but very firmly, told Hillary to meet him in his office in ten minutes.

After ensuring that her phone was forwarded to voice mail, Hillary jogged up to Dr. Westland's office on the fourth floor. Seated opposite Jim, looking out his window toward the Metro North station, Hillary spent several seconds wishing she could get on a train that would take her far away from this discussion. After exchanging the usual pleasantries, Jim got right to the point. He explained that he'd been growing increasingly concerned about Hillary's well being. He'd noticed that Hillary had been calling in sick far too often over the past few months. The results of her latest employment physical were, quite frankly, alarming.

Hillary wished that he, and everyone else, for that matter, would stop badgering her. She felt terrific. True, she had some abdominal pain and bloating during the day, but most women had to learn to live with such discomfort. Her blood pressure was a bit low, but that ran in her family. Her complexion was fine—maybe her skin was just a little dry, but that was probably due to the change in the weather. She wasn't losing as much of her light brown hair as usual—the hair loss would definitely stop once she found a better shampoo, and the shine would return with a new conditioner. Maybe she should switch to that new line of Revlon hair care products. And her smile…people often used to comment on her pretty smile. The bleeding gums were just temporary, most likely the result of having the wrong kind of bristles on the toothbrush she had been using.

Hillary did not see why all these well-meaning people couldn't mind their own damn business. In fact, if they looked in the mirror, several of those who criticized her most would see that they themselves could stand to lose a few pounds. Like her friend Giselle, for one. Giselle used to work as a lingerie model before she had her children. She probably had soared up to 115 pounds since her "retirement" from the runway. Obviously Giselle just didn't have Hillary's will power.

Anyone could see that Hillary looked fabulous. She had to have her clothes custom made because stores just didn't carry a selection for someone with her unique bone structure, and Hillary was tired of shopping in the children's section of *Nordstrom's*. After all, she worked extremely hard to keep trim and was entitled to a wardrobe that flattered her svelte figure.

Each day, Hillary rose religiously at 5:00 a.m. and quietly tiptoed downstairs to the home gym she and her husband Bradford had installed in the basement. They used to work out together, but Brad had quickly lost interest and couldn't maintain the same commitment as she to a rigorous daily workout program. Hillary followed a strict regimen she had developed over time. Recently she had read a study in her *Forty & Fit* magazine, which she had dutifully purchased to support the 7th grade trip to Williamsburg, that having muscle burns more calories. Keeping this latest research in mind, Hillary now began her morning program with several free-weight exercises; then moved over to the flat, incline and decline benches; and finished up the weight-training portion of her workout on the nautilus machines.

After a quick break for mineral water, Hillary started the cardiovascular segment of her training by using the Stairmaster (on Mondays, Wednesdays and Fridays), or the stationary bike (on Tuesdays and Thursdays). She ended each session with 25 minutes on the new elliptical cross trainer she had bought herself for her 40th birthday.

Feeling "forty & fit" after her regimen, Hillary would climb the stairs to the third floor. On most days, her bedroom was now empty, as Brad would already have left to catch his train into Manhattan. She usually had just enough time to wake Tyler so he could start getting ready for school, while she headed to the master bathroom to quickly shower and get dressed for work.

Hillary loved weekend mornings when she had even more time for her workout. She didn't have to be at the hospital on Saturday or Sunday, so rain or shine, Hillary went over to the school track right after her at-home workout. Brad always gave Tyler a big pancake breakfast, which they both loved, but which made her gag, so it really was better for everyone if Hillary had a few hours to herself. Besides, if she didn't take advantage of that extra time on weekends, how would she ever be able to maintain her desired weight?

Brad had stopped complaining that Hillary never had breakfast with Ty; in fact, he had stopped expecting her to have dinner with him as well. He could not understand how she could be satisfied with a plate of various kinds of "rabbit food" garnished with a slice of lemon. Men—they just didn't get it, did they?

And now Westland was pressuring her to meet with Dr. Jonathan Edelstein for some further tests. Dr. Edelstein! For heaven's sake, Edelstein was an endocrinologist. Hillary definitely did not need to go through a battery of tests—she knew she did not have a T-3 deficiency, or abnormal calcium levels. Jim also thought Hillary should see Miriam Rayburn. Hillary was certain that there was nothing wrong with her that warranted a visit to an internist. Rayburn would pressure her to have a lot of unnecessary tests, like a colonoscopy. Even if the Fleets Phosphosoda prep for the test *was* sugar free, Hillary would not endure that unpleasant procedure unless it was absolutely necessary, and she knew that it was not necessary.

And Hillary would know. Before switching to hospital administration, Hillary had been a Registered Nurse (and obscenely overweight at 112 pounds). Thank heavens she had made the career switch to a job in which she could use her medical training, but not have to deal with the day-to-day patient contact. With her current responsibilities at Lawrence Hospital, Hillary could exercise more control over things—pre-certification of insurance, patient and therapist scheduling, monitoring of the physical therapy equipment, claims follow-up...These were areas in which Hillary could demonstrate her excellent organizational and managerial abilities. But Hillary hadn't forgotten everything she had learned in nursing school—she would know if she needed these ridiculous tests. She was fine. Everything was fine. Yes, everything was just fine.

After vague assurances to Jim that she would schedule some appointments as soon as there were openings, Hillary excused herself and raced back to the 2nd floor. Back in her office, her co-workers had pressed for details about the meeting with Dr. Westland, since he rarely made such unscheduled visits. She had reassured her colleagues with a radiant smile and told them that everything was fine. Just fine. In fact, better than fine.

At least the book club meeting would take her mind off the day. If Hillary hurried through these last four laps at the track, she could still get home in time to bake some double-fudge brownies for the group. Maybe she would make some cranberry muffins as well. Since so many of the women at the meeting would be coming straight from their offices, Hillary thought maybe she should make a bread-and-cheese dish too. If she really picked up the pace, Hillary would have time to make dinner for Brad and Ty to eat while she baked. She might be a little late, but it would be worth it. Hillary so enjoyed watching the others eat her homemade creations.

"It isn't necessary to be rich and famous to be happy. It's only necessary to be rich."

Alan Alda

Chapter 5

Carole

christmascarole@eventplanning.org

The phone was ringing as she turned her key in the door. As soon as Carole recognized the voice, she was sorry she had not let the answering machine pick up. It was Andrew's ex-wife, Alexandra, with yet another of her unreasonable demands.

Wasn't it enough that Alexandra was occupying the enormous, beautifully-furnished Victorian home on Sunset and Paradise—perfect name for a perfect street—while Carole and Andrew were crammed into the Lilliputian apartment on Sagamore? What more could that woman possibly want? With the obscene amount of money Alexandra had forced Andrew to spend on attorneys throughout the protracted divorce negotiations, Andrew and Carole could have been living in that stone manor house on Tanglewylde that Carole had her eye on. But it really was true that "Hell hath no fury like a woman scorned."

Like all good fairy tales, the night Carole and Andrew met was memorable. Andrew Grayson was seated next to Carole at the annual dinner dance fundraiser she chaired for the Westchester Arts Council. He was with Alexandra, and truth be told, they made a stunning couple. Heads still turned when the 6'3" Andrew entered a room with the tall, lithe, white-blonde Alexandra on his arm. Andrew and Alexandra had been married for sixteen years and had two beautiful daughters—Mackenzie and Courtney—now twelve and fifteen. But it was obvious to all those who knew the Graysons well that their marriage was in trouble. They were trying to keep up their social commitments as a couple, but the strain was definitely beginning to show.

Throughout the dinner Andrew listened with rapt attention as Carole told him all about herself and the myriad fundraising projects in which she was involved. When he asked how he could become more involved with the Council, she invited him to lunch at *The Town Tavern* on Kraft Avenue so that they could discuss it further. Given Andrew's job as an entertainment attorney, Carole thought that perhaps there was an opportunity for some of his clients to get more involved with the Council.

While they didn't get very far in developing synergies between his clients and the Arts Council, they did develop some synergies of their own. Six short months later, just after Carole's Christmas birthday, Andrew had moved his things out of the house on Sunset & Paradise and into her two-bedroom apartment on Sagamore. That was three years ago, and Andrew's divorce had only just become final—and Andrew and Carole were still in the tiny two-bedroom apartment, in a building with no elevator, no reserved parking…

The living situation was untenable. Andrew's two daughters were loath to spend the weekend in such cramped quarters when they had their own large, private bedroom suites only blocks away. They clearly loved their father, and barely tolerated her, and wanted to spend more time alone with him. Well, Carole also wanted to spend more time alone with Andrew. The girls were just going to have to get used to the fact that, like it or not, Carole was here to stay. If they wanted to be with him, then they would have to understand that she was part of the deal. Carole was tired of trying to win them over, and she strongly believed that if Alexandra had done a better job of parenting them, the girls would surely behave more civilly to her. Carole wondered aloud, "Didn't I give up my cherished guestroom so that they could stay over and be near their father?" If they had to abide by her stricter house rules, it was only for their own good, since they so obviously needed discipline. After all she did for Mackenzie and Courtney, Carole felt that they could at least act appreciative.

Carole hoped it would be different when (if?) she had children of her own. As a 34-year-old woman, she was finally coming to grips with the fact that she did not have forever if she wanted to have a child. It didn't make her feel particularly optimistic when the book club discussed Sylvia Ann Hewlett's book *Creating a Life: Professional Women and the Quest for Children*. On an intellectual level, Carole understood Hewlett's finding that 42% of professional women have no children by aged 40, since these women typically marry men who already have children and don't want any more. On an emotional level, it was a difficult pill to swallow.

Fifteen years her senior, Andrew had always been up front with her that while he understood her desire for a baby, he just couldn't handle the additional emotional and financial responsibility another child would bring. He loved her with all his heart and would do almost anything for her, but he couldn't commit to having another child. He was having a difficult enough time parenting Mackenzie and Courtney, dealing with his ex-wife Alexandra, paying for two households, and building what he hoped would be a long-term relationship with Carole. A new baby would just about push him over the edge. Was that what she wanted?

Alexandra's phone call just now had been to inform Carole, "Andrew *must* take the girls tonight since something important came up, and I have to catch the 5:16 into Grand Central. I have a dinner engagement with friends and won't be home until quite late. Tell Andrew he has to make sure the girls come straight over to the apartment after field hockey and get started on their homework. And this time, make sure he remembers to check Mackenzie's Math assignment. He obviously didn't check it the last time Mackenzie was over, and she did not do well on her quiz. Perhaps if Andrew had done what he was supposed to do, the girls wouldn't be having so much difficulty at school." As Carole held the phone away from her ear, she didn't hear the remaining diatribe on all the other ways in which Andrew was failing in his parental duties.

On the bright side, the girls would be tickled that Carole wouldn't be home tonight. Her book club meeting was at 7:30, and she had no intention of missing it. She had to prove to Andrew that she really was making an effort with these women, even though she didn't seem to have much in common with any of them. Last month, when Carole had expressed her desire to drop out of the club, Andrew quickly reminded her that he had

had to call in quite a few favors just to get her into the group. Andrew had some well intentioned (but definitely erroneous) notion that women like Sarah or Madison could help Carole better understand how to deal with Mackenzie and Courtney, and the issues they faced growing up in a small, wealthy suburb like Bronxville.

Carole, however, saw things a bit differently. She thought that even though she was the only member of the group who did not have children of her own, the others would benefit more from listening to her unique perspective on child rearing than she would gain from hearing about their experiences. Often it appeared that they did not appreciate her views, but clearly they needed to hear from someone who was as objective as she. After all, she had read so many books on parenting for that Women's Studies course she had taken at the New School. She had even received a B+ on her final exam. Between her coursework and her experiences as a stepparent to two girls that Alexandra spoiled outrageously, Carole could obviously bring more impartiality to the subject of raising children in Bronxville.

Her mind came back to having a child of her own—as it did more and more frequently these days. If Carole did have a baby, and it was looking like a very big "if" at this point, she knew she would never make the kinds of mistakes that Alexandra or some of the women in her book club seemed to make. Why did they make parenting seem so difficult? Maybe not Francesca so much, she seemed like a pretty good mother. But some of those other women…

Carole ran her fingers through her shoulder length auburn hair and sighed. It was getting late and she needed to get ready for book club. She'd better call Andrew and let him know the latest development with Alexandra. He would not be amused.

Some fairy tale…

Carole couldn't help but wonder, "Would they live happily ever after?"

"There are three good reasons to be a teacher—June, July, and August."

Unknown

Chapter 6

Francesca

maestramama@westchesterteachers.edu

The school year was almost over and Francesca was delighted with how well her new job had turned out. She knew how fortunate she was to even get the part-time Teacher's Aide appointment for the Bronxville Middle School Spanish program. When she had initially applied for the position, Francesca saw it as a nice re-entry to the workforce she had willingly left after her son Nicholas was born. She could use her native language skills in an environment she loved. The kids were high spirited, but generally well-behaved and eager to learn. Several of them had told Francesca she looked just like Catherine Zeta Jones, so they were obviously very bright.

Her commute was a dream. Although her colleagues had to arrive well before classes started to vie for the limited parking spaces, Francesca simply stepped out of her townhouse at Bolton Gardens and crossed over Pondfield Road to the main entrance of the school. Each morning she walked by the pathway embedded with bricks bearing the names of many of the graduates of the Bronxville School. She smiled when she passed the brick she and her husband Robert had bought for Nicholas as a graduation present.

Francesca was quite familiar with The Bronxville School from her many years as a volunteer in all three schools—elementary, middle and high—which were all housed in one handsome building. When Nicholas was young, Francesca had jumped at the chance to be class mother for his 2nd grade class. By the time he was in the 3rd grade, she had taken on the challenge of running the Elementary School Book Fair. When he entered 4th, she oversaw the Publishing Center, and by 5th she was coordinating the Chat 'N Chew Reading lunchtime reading program. As soon as Nicholas started 6th grade, Francesca volunteered to be the PTA Middle School Liaison; 7th brought her responsibility for the Teen Center, and by 8th grade Francesca was elected Middle School Chair. During Nicholas' High School years, she was a proud Drama Mama, Spanish Club special trips' chauffeur, and editor of the Bronxville School directory. Her final bittersweet duty was to plan the menu and seating for the Scholastic Achievement Dinner held at the Field Club to honor outstanding seniors. Thank goodness she hadn't volunteered to supervise the Yearbook Committee during Nicholas' senior year—the infamous year in which the editors were not allowed to participate in the much-anticipated graduation ceremony. Of course, that whole debacle made the papers and the Channel 12 news. After all, this was Bronxville.

With unemployment levels so high, Francesca was happy she had been able to find any job, never mind one working with some of the best educators in what was indisputably one of the finest school districts in the nation. The class sizes were small, and the courses challenging. Since the village itself was so small, the elementary, middle and high school kids all streamed throughout the wings of the same building. The building might look a little tired on the inside, and badly in need of a facelift, but as one of Nicholas' former teachers proved, a facelift wasn't always an improvement.

While Francesca wished her position were full time, she understood that it would take a few more years before the elementary school children participating in the new Foreign Language curriculum moved up into the Middle School. The Administrators were doing their best to hold down the budget increases and were unable to justify an increase in her duties. But they encouraged her to hang in there…it would happen.

When she first saw the ad for the *paid* teaching spot, Francesca applied immediately. After many years of unpaid volunteer positions in all three schools, she had worn out her joke that she had received a 10% annual increase in her salary. Her mathematically gifted son would always counter that 10% of $0 was still zero! Her teaching stipend would at least make a small dent in Nicholas' escalating college tuition bills.

Now at MIT, Nicholas was applying himself to his studies and making high honors in an extremely rigorous program. Of course, Francesca and Robert did not delude themselves that Nicholas was at the library every Friday and Saturday night. He had introduced them to a new girlfriend who attended a nearby school, and they seemed pretty serious.

Francesca and Robert had always thought they had saved more than enough to cover Nicholas' tuition for the four years it would take him to earn his undergraduate degree. However, with the economy in turmoil, the capital gains on which they had counted had been completely decimated.

If only Robert's business would bounce back. Any financial cushion they had amassed was disappearing rapidly. Over the last twenty years, Francesca had witnessed first-hand Robert's hard work building his executive search firm into one of the most highly regarded firms on the street. Specializing in the financial services industry, Robert was no stranger to downturns in the economy and high unemployment levels. His business had survived tough times in the 80's and the recession in the early 90's, but Robert confided in her that he had never felt as pessimistic as he did now.

No one on Wall Street was hiring. At all.

Robert's phone rang constantly, but unfortunately it was from friends and business contacts that found themselves out of work, the latest casualties of yet another "rightsizing" in the financial services community. White-collar professionals were being laid off in record numbers—these were the same professionals who only a few short years ago Robert had placed in senior positions, with significant sign-on bonuses and highly creative compensation packages.

Colleagues who called Robert were dealing with uncharted circumstances. On top of their already-high monthly payments for dual mortgages, property taxes, car loans, and household staff, they were now receiving the first tuition bills for their oldest children. For many of these executives, their severance packages were coming to an end, but they had yet to secure new positions. While Robert truly sympathized with their plight, at least they had severance. Robert was painfully aware that no corporate power was going to award him two-to-four weeks' salary for every year of service, and continued medical coverage for his family.

Francesca wished she could do more. Friends wanted to help; that is, those few friends in whom Robert agreed she could confide. But in this crazy economic environment, there was only so much they could do. Perhaps at the book club meeting tonight she could speak with Sarah. While they only knew each other from the book club, Sarah was the Human Resources Director for the Corporate Finance area of one of the major banks. Francesca couldn't remember which one—with all the Bank mergers, she couldn't keep track of what any of them were called these days. Robert had mentioned on several occasions that he'd been trying for years to get a foot in the door of Sarah's bank. It might be awkward, but Francesca would talk to her to see if she could meet with Robert. At this point, pride was a luxury they simply couldn't afford.

Francesca glanced up at the Seth Thomas School House clock her mother had given them for their first anniversary. She was shocked to see that it was 7:23 already. (If only the clock had come equipped with a school bell!) She quickly finished up her Pasta with Shrimp and put the leftovers in a Tupperware container for when Robert came home later.

Francesca grabbed her book, shoulder bag, and car keys from the table and hurried out the door. She would hate to be marked "Tardy"!

"When I read about the evils of drinking, I gave up reading."

Henny Youngman

Chapter 7

Sarah

inhumanresource@womeninbanking.com

Sarah scrambled down the escalator at Grand Central Station and scanned the big board for the departure gate for the 6:38 Harlem Line train to Bronxville. The good news was that the train hadn't departed yet; the bad news was that it was leaving from Track 110 downstairs. Sarah pushed through the crowd and bounded down the steps. She could see that the door to the ramp leading to the train was still open. She flew to the ramp and arrived in time to see the rear lights of the train as it pulled out. Damn. Now she would be late for the meeting tonight. She could get the 7:05 that got into Bronxville at 7:32, but she wouldn't have time to stop off at home to see Roger and the kids and grab a bottle of wine to bring to the meeting.

Thinking about the wine, Sarah decided she might as well have a quick drink at the *Oyster Bar* while she waited for the next train. It might help her to relax after a particularly stressful day.

When had they taken the "human" out of Human Resources? As a Senior HR Director, Sarah knew all the theories that you shouldn't fire someone on a Friday—best to do it on a Thursday. Who even remembered why that was. In this day and age, terminations occurred every day of the week, even during the holidays, once a sacred time in her human resources career. The people on the Media and Telecommunications team they had let go today had joined JP Morgan Chase Bank only two years ago. With the Bank taking loan loss provisions for the majority of the team's portfolio, and no new deals in the pipeline, it was time for the Bank to cut their losses and eliminate the group. Although Sarah had been through this drill more times than she cared to think about during her working life, she still could not help but get a knot in her stomach over what she had to do as professionally and humanely as possible.

Sarah entered the dimly lit *Oyster Bar* and found a spot alone at a small table just inside the door. As she set down her overstuffed briefcase, and loosened the Hermès scarf that no longer looked casually draped over her shoulders, a waiter approached with a smile and asked if she wanted her usual. Her usual? Was she really becoming that much of a regular? Sarah didn't think she particularly stood out in a crowd. As a blonde-haired, blue-eyed woman of average height and weight, she generally felt quite anonymous in Bronxville—a town that seemed to have more than its fair share of women with her coloring.

Drink in hand, Sarah replayed the events of the day, events that were becoming more and more the norm. "Here's your package...Please let me know if you have any questions...Call your outplacement counselor at Lee Hecht Harrison to make an appointment as soon as possible...No, there's nothing you can do to change the decision...I'm sorry, but we don't have any other positions for someone with your background and experience...Yes, you must leave today." Sarah was finding it harder and harder to laugh at the play on words when friends asked if she worked in "Inhuman Resources."

These days Sarah's usual high volume of e-mail and voice mail messages almost never contained any good news. Dealing with employee morale issues, investigating sexual harassment complaints, conferring with outside legal counsel on termination agreements, consulting with the Bank's Employee Assistance Program, attending unemployment disputes, and holding ongoing meetings with managers to determine the next round of layoffs—that was now the norm. What had happened to the days when her calendar was filled with interview appointments and lunches with managers to strategize on how they could grow their businesses with the best and the brightest? It seemed like a lifetime ago that Sarah had pushed for new programs to recruit and retain staff—flextime, telecommuting, and performance bonuses. Now she was tasked with eliminating these same programs as the Bank exhorted the "lucky" staff members who remained to do more with less.

Lost in her reverie, Sarah was shocked that it was 7:10. She had missed the express train. Now she would have to take the 7:30 local. Sarah signaled the waiter for another drink before pulling out her Blackberry—eleven new messages. Scanning the items, she decided that all of them could hold until tomorrow when she was better able to respond. She might as well check her cell phone too. Only 4 messages—one of them from Madison, asking if she would be at the meeting tonight.

Sarah missed seeing Madison on the train ride into Grand Central each morning. As two of the few working mothers on the hushed 6:56 a.m. train (not the more social 8:44!), they had fallen into an easy routine that made the commute so much more bearable. After a quick update on the latest personal news, they separated Madison's *New York Times*. Once they finished their respective sections—Sarah started with the International and National News, while Madison went right to Business and Metro—they wordlessly exchanged papers. Neither cared for Sports, which went unread into the recycling bin as they exited the train. Sarah was finding it increasingly difficult to get out of bed each morning to make that train.

Why was she finding it so hard to get her act together lately? She had dealt with hundreds of tough challenges in her career…She could handle these latest stresses. As her son Dylan said, "No big."

If she hurried, at least Sarah would see Madison and the others at the meeting tonight. She hadn't actually read the book that they would be talking about tonight—in fact, now that she thought about it, she hadn't even bought the book—but she knew she would enjoy the discussion. Sarah's dirty little secret used to be that she would read every one of the novels recommended by Oprah. She had been extremely disappointed when Oprah discontinued her book club after being insulted by an author who was less than thrilled with the *Oprah Book Club* imprimatur on his book. In Sarah's opinion, Oprah had an uncanny ability to pick books that portrayed every conceivable dysfunctional family. Books like *White Oleander; Vinegar Hill; Black and Blue;* and *The Pilot's Wife* provided a much-needed escape from the "real" dysfunction Sarah had to deal with

"I have been complimented many times
and they always embarrass me; I always
feel that they have not said enough."

Mark Twain

Chapter 8

Giselle

modelcitizen @thelingerielady.com

*H*e was a bodice ripper; she was a print model. Massimo was someone for whom the description "tall, dark and handsome" was invented; Giselle was breathtakingly blonde and beautiful. Massimo and Giselle met during a photo shoot in Manhattan—he was posing for the cover of the latest Barbara Cartland novel; she was in town for a *Vogue* layout featuring the latest creations of the lingerie line she was representing. Each was extremely successful and sought after in their individual careers.

That was fourteen years and two children ago. Still a striking couple, the number of photo shoots had diminished as the competition from younger models increased dramatically, but Massimo and Giselle progressed happily into the next phase of their lives.

It had been an almost seamless process for Massimo to transition into a career for the "more mature" male model. Men developed more "character" as they aged. Giselle was happy she was no longer being asked to pose in those unbearably tight, skimpy, see-through pieces of fabric that passed for articles of clothing. It was almost by accident that she had stumbled into her current career consulting on the design of the lingerie pieces she had once modeled. One of her favorite manufacturers, tired of her endless complaints about the garments, had dared her to design something sexy *and* comfortable. Giselle did, and the rest, as they say, was history.

Given the nature of their business, both Massimo and Giselle had some flexibility in arranging their schedules so that one of them was always home after school. Their two girls, Hannah and Lily, were in the Bronxville Elementary School and involved, it seemed, in every conceivable activity the town had to offer. There always seemed to be a Girl Scout meeting to organize, museum trip to chaperone, soccer practice to coach, music lesson to supervise, ballet class to provide a ride for, or birthday party to either buy a present for/drive to/pick up from/or host. On Wednesdays, Hannah attended *Miss Covington's School of Dance & Etiquette,* while Lily was tutored on the piano.

Giselle was so happy Kindergarten was behind them. Without a full-day kindergarten program at the school, coordinating the pick-up schedules for both girls had been a nightmare. This week, pick-up was a little less hectic since the second graders, including their Lily, were away for three days on the traditional farm trip. Hannah, their fourth grader, was enjoying being the "only child" and had told Giselle she wouldn't mind if the class stayed away for just a few more days.

Since it was Thursday, Giselle was planning her day to "work" at home after the morning drop-off at school:

♦ enroll in the advanced yoga class at the Bronxville Athletic Club;

♦ attend conference with Lily's Spanish tutor at 9:30;

♦ shop for ingredients to bake Blueberry Cobbler for Memorial Day Bake Sale—add 10 points for homemade, instead of from a mix!;

♦ stop by *Try & Buy* for 2 birthday party gifts;

♦ get a haircut at *Studio One*;

♦ meet with other fourth grade Moms for lunch to discuss appropriate sleep away camps for the summer—is Hannah ready???;

♦ pick up dry cleaning at *Spic and Span*;

♦ get to Library Lane by 2:10 to find parking spot in time for 2:40 pick-up;

♦ drop Hannah at Victoria's house at 3:15 for a play date;

♦ zip up to *Lord & Taylor* to see if they have any new taffeta dresses for Lily and Hannah to wear to the Piano Recital in two weeks;

♦ purchase a new battery for Lily's cell phone at *Worldwide Wireless Communications.*

♦ pick Hannah up at 5:15 and swing by *Value Drugs* to pick out some materials for the girls to decorate their bikes for the Memorial Day parade. Also check *Fierson's* for party dresses if *Lord & Taylor* is a bust.

So much for free time. Giselle thought that her being at home three days a week, with Massimo covering the other two, would make things run much more smoothly in their household. Even with a cleaning lady, gardener, and roster of part-time babysitters, there never seemed to be enough hands to get things done. With several deadlines hanging over her head— she still needed to finish the preliminary designs for the new tap pants and camisole set—Giselle debated whether or not to attend tonight's book club meeting. She had some creative ideas for fabric and cut that she really should work on, but she was finding it hard to find a block of uninterrupted time so she could concentrate. Since Giselle knew she wouldn't get much uninterrupted time at home, she convinced herself that she might as well enjoy a night with her book club!

That reminded her of one more thing to feel guilty about—she hadn't finished the book they were planning to discuss tonight. Giselle had thought she'd have plenty of time this week to catch up on her reading, what with Lily being away on the farm trip, but somehow the time had evaporated. Maybe while she was parked at the library waiting for Hannah she could make a respectable dent in the first few chapters.

At least this book club was a bit more relaxed than one of the others in town Giselle had tried to join—"Sorry, we're not accepting any new members!" From what her neighbor Schyuler told her, you dared not be late, and you dared not show up unprepared for those book club meetings. Each month a new leader was chosen who was responsible for researching the book and the author, thereby guaranteeing a very productive and serious discussion. Reading lists were disseminated to all members promptly—Oprah need not apply. Missing a meeting was strongly frowned upon and grounds for an invitation to withdraw from the book club.

Lifting the portable phone from its cradle in the kitchen, Giselle dialed Kathryn's office. She went straight to voice mail. "Sorry I haven't called sooner, Kathryn…I'll be there tonight…Let me know if you need me to bring anything." Next Giselle tried to reach Hillary at the hospital, but she wasn't picking up. Giselle just left a brief message asking Hillary if she would like a ride to the meeting.

Hopefully Hillary would check her voice mail before she left the hospital and accept Giselle's offer of a ride. Giselle wanted to get a few words alone with her tonight. Over her years in the fashion industry, Giselle had worked with too, too many women who had starved themselves to fit into the designer samples. Giselle was blessed with fabulous metabolism and knew how lucky she was never to have had a weight problem herself. She also felt fortunate that healthy-looking models were the rage when she was at the peak of her career. She never felt the need to starve herself to Kate Moss proportions. Hillary, on the other hand, could give Calista Flockhart a run for her money—she clearly she needed help, and Giselle hoped Hillary would be open to her overtures.

Even without Lily in the house, it was still taking the family much too long to get going this morning. Giselle called up the stairs to Massimo and Hannah. "C'mon you guys, I need to drop you off on my way to the Athletic Club and I don't want us all to be late. Massimo, if you don't hurry you're going to miss the 8:04. Hannah, don't forget to bring down your violin. You have orchestra today."

Giselle adjusted her smooth, pocketless yoga leggings and grabbed her car keys and tote bag. She threw in a copy of the book for the meeting tonight. It was possible she'd get to read a bit of it today, in between errands. Not likely, of course, but possible.

"There is never enough time,

unless you're serving it."

Malcolm Forbes

Chapter 9

Chelsea

greenthum@graciousgardens.com

Chelsea was exhausted. Absolutely exhausted. The diminutive, chestnut haired dynamo felt as though her gas tank was on "E." Even if her husband Ted managed to get home in time to stay with the boys, she wasn't sure if she would have the energy to make it to the book club meeting tonight.

Her work with the Grand Central Business Improvement district was so rewarding, but so draining. As a native New Yorker, Chelsea was thrilled when midtown property owners created this partnership to revitalize the neighborhood around the landmark Grand Central Terminal. Their ambitious $30 million capital improvements plan—new street furniture, lights and traffic signals; handicapped-accessible street corners; and frequent cultivation, maintenance and replacement of trees, sidewalks planters and hanging baskets—was such a wonderful idea that had been long overdue in her beloved Manhattan. Chelsea's latest sidewalk plantings of bright yellow daffodils and deep purple hyacinths were drawing rave reviews in the city.

Chelsea was also finishing up her spring course at the Bronxville Adult School. The women in her "Introduction to Landscaping" class were a wonderful group who really wanted to soak up as much information as they could to improve their own gardens. Many of them, their children grown and out of the house, had now turned their many talents to the nurturing of their gardens. They asked so many questions!!! They were already pressuring Chelsea to teach a more advanced class in the fall.

And of course there were her labors of love with the Bronxville Beautification Committee, of which she was a charter member. She had just completed organizing and participating in several of the many botanical events that took place during the annual Beautification Week. It was a true pleasure to be involved with the legion of volunteers who fanned out through the community to lend their special talents to keeping their village in pristine condition. She just wished she had time to keep her own yard in such pristine condition!

Chelsea was also involved with the Bronxville Chamber of Commerce that so generously sponsored the flower boxes that store patrons enjoyed as they shopped and strolled down Pondfield Road. She tried to carve out time to help the Chamber with each season's plantings, but the seasons seemed to be coming much more quickly these days. Thank goodness Chelsea would have a break before the holiday decorations needed to be planned!

In addition to all those "outside" activities, Chelsea certainly couldn't neglect her private landscape consulting business. Not surprisingly, this was one of her busiest times of the year. She knew she should be grateful that she lived in a community where despite the general downturn in the economy, the residents were still interested in hiring her to beautify every inch of their well-maintained properties. Even with the seasonal part-time staff she had taken on, Chelsea could barely keep up with the demand for her services. As Ted reminded her, this dilemma fell squarely under the "Good Problem" column.

With summer approaching, Chelsea was looking forward to a slight lull in her activities so she could spend more unstructured time with her sons Michael and Lucas. Lucas would be having his "Moving Up" ceremony from 5th grade in June. He couldn't wait to get to the 6th grade where he would have a combination locker; change classrooms and teachers throughout the day; and best of all, walk into the village for lunch, just as his older brother Michael had done. (Unfortunately, with all the construction problems, not having a cafeteria had turned a privilege into a necessity.) As an eighth-grader in the Middle School, Michael was looking forward to finishing his Regents exams and graduating to the High School.

High School...Chelsea didn't even want to think about everything that went along with having a son in high school—driving, later curfews, dating!

For the present, Chelsea knew she would not be able to accomplish even half of what she did without the support of her father-in-law, Joseph Hollingsworth. She and Ted both knew how lucky they were that Joseph, a retired Economics professor, was so involved in their children's lives. At their ages, Michael and Lucas most definitely did not want a "baby" sitter. In actuality, what they really needed was someone to pick them up from school, drive them to their innumerable activities, and help them with their increasingly challenging homework assignments. Grandpa J fit the bill perfectly. He had even mastered the confusing 6-day cycle so he always knew which child had which classes on any given day.

A widower, Joseph had finally agreed to sell his house on Kensington Road and move into Chelsea and Ted's home only one year ago. Chelsea blessed the day he moved in. In previous years, when asked by Ted what she would like for Christmas, Chelsea had always responded that she wanted only two things—a House Elf and a Wife. She dreamed about what she could get done if she had one of Harry Potter's house elves that served the family to which they were "bound", doing all the menial tasks and creating fabulous meals. And a wife...someone who would take care of the children in a way that lived up to Chelsea's impossible standards. On Christmas morning, Chelsea would feign disappointment when she opened all her presents and didn't get the "gifts" she had requested.

Now, Chelsea had nothing to complain about. She didn't get the House Elf or a wife, but she had gotten something much more meaningful for her family. Joseph was a true gift not only to her and Ted, but also to the boys who greatly benefited from his companionship and guidance. Chelsea liked to think she was good in Math, but she was no match for Joseph. She wasn't sure how the boys would have fared meeting all the rigorous state testing requirements that had recently been put in place without their grandfather's one-on-one tutoring sessions.

With all Joseph did for the family during the day while she and Ted were at work, Chelsea hated to ask him to stay with the kids tonight so she could go to the book club meeting. She knew he wouldn't mind, but she didn't want to take advantage of his unfailing good nature. She called Ted at his office and left a voice mail asking him to please catch the early train so he could take over supervision of the boy's homework. If Ted could get home before 7:30, Chelsea could still make the meeting.

In the meantime, if she really concentrated, she could probably find the strength to read at least the book jacket of *I Don't Know How She Does It: The Life of Kate Reddy, Working Mother.* Chelsea hadn't a clue how Kate did it, but she would dearly love to find out.

"Money can't buy happiness;
it can, however, rent it."

Anonymous

Chapter 10

Madison

munnyhunny@jaegerwood.com

nless she could convince the group to change the night of
their meetings, this would probably be Madison's last time
participating in the book club. Since some of the School
Board meetings had been moved from Mondays to Thursdays, Madison
had been forced to make some changes in her personal life. The book club
was one of the few social commitments Madison had allowed herself, and
alas, that was now on the endangered list.

Her partners at Jaeger, Wood & Fenwick continued to be extremely
understanding and supportive. Before running for the School Board,
Madison had consulted with them and negotiated how she would split her
time between her clients and her Board responsibilities, and secured their
100% buy in. Her family had also signed on, but the long hours were
beginning to take their toll.

As a long-time Bronxville resident and member of the 13-year club
(made up of those who had attended the Bronxville School from
Kindergarten through 12th grade), Madison was passionate about giving
back to her community and ensuring that her own children benefited from
the very best the school could offer. She had been encouraged to run for
the School Board, but the process to get elected was not for the faint of
heart. After numerous interviews with the Bronxville Committee for the
Non Partisan Nomination and Election of School Trustees (NPC), and an
extensive check of her references, the Committee endorsed Madison for

one of the two open seats. After winning by a respectable margin, she proudly took her place at the table with her fellow Board members.

Madison had to admit that she knew what she was getting into—construction, construction, and more construction issues.

As far back as 1999, the Bronxville community had overwhelmingly supported the $22 million bond referendum for an attractive three-story addition to meet the burgeoning enrollment. By 2000, when disgruntled union workers displayed a large gray rat adjacent to the school playing fields, village residents were treated to a visible reminder that the project had careened wildly off track. In 2001, the community not so overwhelmingly approved another $6 million for cost overruns to complete the project. With more changes to come and no completion date in sight in 2003, village residents were at the end of their patience.

Madison's family was feeling the strain resulting from the huge time commitment that Board activities demanded—endless reviews of background material related to specific agenda items, weekly visits to the construction site, biweekly televised meetings, intense budget workshops, and numerous phone calls and e-mails from concerned residents. Although Madison was more than willing to take the time to explain her views on a thorny issue or listen to a neighbor's concern about the budget, it never ceased to amaze her when an elementary school mother approached her for help getting a certain teacher for her child. She literally had to bite her tongue as she suggested it might be best if they simply wrote a letter to the principal and hoped for the best.

John, Madison's husband, was trying to pick up the slack at home, but there was just so much going on. Their son Cole was a junior, arguably one of the most important years of his school career thus far. John was shouldering the burden of driving Cole to college visits in the New England area and ensuring that he participated in the right SAT tutoring programs in town. Of course, Madison hoped Cole would continue the family tradition and matriculate at either Yale or Princeton, but she felt guilty that she was relying on John to guide their son through the whole application process.

Madison treasured her once-a-month book club meetings both for the social outlet as well as the opportunity to hear what people in the town were talking about. In a real life version of the telephone game, Madison was constantly amazed at how a story about something she knew for a fact was going on in the school could be totally transformed by the time the story made its way back to her. If only she could harness the power of this unbelievable grapevine!

It was 6:23 p.m. and she was still trying to get out of her office to make the train. Several times she had started to leave, only to be called back for just one more phone call that couldn't wait. With determination, Madison stuffed a folder into her tote, waved goodnight to her assistant, and headed out the heavy wooden doors of her firm. She rang for the elevator and waited. Adjusting her position in front of the highly polished chrome elevator doors, she tried to see if her dark brown hair was at least somewhat in place. Before she could get a good look, a soft "Ping" signaled the arrival of the next car. Stepping into the empty elevator, she pushed "L" and tried calling Sarah on her cell phone one more time to see if she would be on the 6:38 train. Still no answer.

Madison was becoming more and more concerned about Sarah. They had met at the "Making Strides Against Breast Cancer" fund-raising walk two years ago. She and Sarah hit it off so well that they continued walking together at the school track on weekends when their hectic schedules allowed, and they sat together on the 6:56 morning train into Grand Central. Lately Sarah had not been at the track, nor had she been on their usual train as frequently as she had been in the past.

Madison was no shrink—and that heavens for that since she thought they were all a bit crazy themselves!—but the few times she had seen Sarah in the past few weeks, Madison felt that Sarah seemed to be a bit depressed, not her usual upbeat self. Sarah didn't seem to be coping well with the incredible stresses of her job. She might also be starting to get a little sad about her daughter's imminent departure for college. It had to be tough to let your "baby" go. Madison made a mental note to get Sarah aside at the meeting tonight to see if there was anything she could do.

Settling her medium frame into the aisle seat on the 6:38 train, Madison reached into her Prada calfskin leather tote and pulled out her monthly commutation pass. After the conductor nodded in her direction and continued moving through the car, Madison reached for two of the manila folders she had brought with her—one marked Jaeger, Wood & Fenwick; the other, The Bronxville School Board of Education—and the hardcover book for tonight's meeting. She couldn't decide if she should review the materials in the folders or start reading the novel. Madison decided she would close her heavy-lidded hazel eyes for just a minute while she made up her mind.

"Bronxville…This station stop is Bronxville…"

Oh my God!

Madison's eyes flew open. She quickly gathered her belongings and joined her weary neighbors lining up to depart the train. She just hoped she would get a second wind before the meeting in less than twenty-five minutes.

"The secret of success is sincerity. Once you can fake that, you've got it made."

Jean Giraudoux

Chapter 11

The Bronxville Book Club

The May Meeting

fter dropping Whitney off at Taylor's house on Avon Road, Lizbet made a right on Midland Avenue and headed over to Masterton. She guided her Midnight Blue Lexus past the stone pillars at the bottom of Kathryn's driveway and pulled up to the front entryway. According to Lizbet's 18K, white-gold Cartier watch, it was 7:30 p.m. on the dot. Perfect! It looked like she was the first of the book club members to arrive. Lizbet pulled down the visor and checked her hair and makeup in the lighted mirror before grabbing her new Louis Vuitton Keepall (with those adorable, confetti-colored logos on a white background), Motorola phone/PDA, and a copy of the book for tonight's discussion. In her haste to be prompt, she had forgotten the scones Mrs. Crawford had baked. Oh well. Lizbet decided that she'd just drop the scones off at the High School Guidance office tomorrow morning. While there, she might as well see if she could find out who else from Bronxville was applying to Yale.

At the massive oak front door, Lizbet rang the deep chimes and waited, expecting Kathryn's fabulous housekeeper Mrs. Crawford to answer the door. When Kathryn appeared, Lizbet remembered that Kathryn had had to let the remarkable Mrs. Crawford go after the divorce. Poor Kathryn.

Kiss...kiss...

"Kathryn, I haven't seen you in ages! Did you do something to your hair? Is it a new color?"

"And that outfit! I love it. I had one just like it...last year."

Lizbet moved into the foyer as Kathryn closed the door and continued her one-sided conversation. "I haven't seen you playing golf lately, where have you been keeping yourself?"

Kathryn invited Lizbet into the great room for something to drink before the others arrived. Kathryn secretly shuddered when she realized just how much she used to be like Lizbet in the years B.D.—*Before Divorce*. Lizbet, who as a Yale co-ed had majored and minored in finding a suitable husband, had never worked a day in her life. When Kathryn first moved to Bronxville as Mrs. P. David Chasen III, she and Lizbet had spent many a day shopping, lunching, or playing a round of golf. Oh how things had changed. Not that Kathryn was exactly coupon cutting.

Before Lizbet's arrival, Kathryn had been in the process of taking the Chardonnay out of the wine cooler that kept the bottles at precisely the ideal temperature (between 50 and 55 degrees Fahrenheit) and checking on the hors d'ouevres for the meeting. She felt fairly confident that everything was pretty much under control by this point, but Lizbet's offer of assistance was appreciated. Kathryn really wanted to like her, but…

While Schubert's String quartet in C major played softly in the background, Kathryn asked Lizbet to uncork the Kendall Jackson. (The way this group emptied wine bottles, she was not about to bring out the Pouilly Fuisse Jadot 2000.) Walking to the other end of the kitchen, Kathryn found some sparkling water and Diet Coke in the spare refrigerator. She artfully arranged the beverages on the sideboard where they would probably remain untouched for the evening. On the other hand, perhaps Hillary would have some of the water. In that case, Kathryn thought she had better slice some lemons too.

With the beverages in place, Kathryn proceeded to remove the cold hors d'ouevres from the Sub-zero and the warm ones from the warming drawer. With an artful touch, she carefully arranged the delicacies on an eclectic array of antique chinaware laid out on the salmon granite countertop. Kathryn hadn't had time to set out the guest's individual serving plates, so she opened the drawer of her new dual dishwasher that held the just-cleaned tableware. With Lizbet's help, she retrieved the stemware from the 16th-century French buffet she and David had picked up in Paris on their last trip before the divorce. Lizbet recognized the wine glasses as the Waterford Glenmore pattern, which had to be specially ordered. She thought about getting a dozen to supplement her own set of hand-cut crystal wine goblets.

Lizbet asked Kathryn where she kept the wine finders. Lizbet adored these fabulous charms that you attached to each guest's glass so she would remember which glass was hers. She especially liked Kathryn's pewter collection that featured sunglasses, nail polish, cell phone, high heel shoe, martini, and shopping bag. After carefully laying out the charms on a white linen placemat next to the stemware, Lizbet removed the shopping bag and placed it on her own glass.

As she sipped her Chardonnay, Lizbet admired the vaulted ceiling and large Palladian window. She walked over towards the window to admire a striking, hand-painted rug that she had not noticed before. "Kathryn, is this new?" Kathryn told her that she had seen one like it a friend's home on Elm Lane, and then convinced David that they just had to have one in their kitchen. The $200,000 plus Kathryn and David had spent two years ago to renovate the kitchen had been worth every penny. Kathryn had taken all the best ideas from the homes Bronxville Real Estate Partners listed, and the results were magnificent, if she did say so herself. Making an effort to be nice, Kathryn asked, "Lizbet, would you like the phone number of the artist who did the floor?"

Before Lizbet could answer, Kathryn heard the door chimes again. Hillary swept into the room. For someone who weighed so little, she certainly knew how to make an entrance. Her arms were overflowing with large packages of food. Who could possibly eat all that? Hillary immediately took over the food preparation from Kathryn so that Kathryn could concentrate on getting her guests settled. The three women heard Francesca coming in the door, calling hello.

Francesca greeted Kathryn and Lizbet and offered to help get things ready, but Hillary had everything under control. Lizbet complimented Francesca on her new haircut and asked after the family. She knew Francesca's son Nicolas was at MIT, so she asked, "Francesca, do you have any advice for me on how to survive the awful college admissions process? Who did you use to write Nicholas' essay for his applications?"

Francesca sometimes ran into Lizbet's daughter, since the elementary, middle and high school were all connected. Francesca knew how much Lizbet's daughter Whitney wanted to go to BU, while her mother and father were pressuring her to apply early decision to Yale. As diplomatically as she could, Francesca tried to suggest to Lizbet that Whitney needed to follow her heart and choose the school that was right for her. As if she didn't hear what Francesca said, Lizbet "joked" about her secret weapon to convince Whitney to apply to Yale—a new, cherry red BMW convertible to take with her to Freshman year in New Haven, *not* Boston.

Before Francesca could say another word, someone called "Anybody home?" After placing a bottle of French Chardonnay on the sideboard, Anne joined the group and politely asked after everyone's welfare. Barely listening to their responses, Anne smiled vacantly while appraising the great room.

As she had confided to Donald on the way over, Anne had been *dying* to get a look at the inside of Kathryn's house. She wouldn't have missed this meeting for anything and couldn't wait to move into the formal living room for the book discussion. Anne made small talk with Kathryn, Hillary, Francesca, and Lizbet while moving around the large kitchen, her blue-grey eyes taking in every detail. After a reminder for all to drop off their baked goods for Memorial Day at the Elementary School canopy, Lizbet excused herself from the group to help Hillary with the food. Lizbet's very dear friends Emma and Allistair Stanford lived on Prescott Avenue, and they were definitely upset about Anne's recent home "improvements." It didn't matter how spectacular the pieces in her boutique were, no one who was anyone was going to cross the threshold of *Annetiques*. Anne didn't seem to know it yet, but she was history in this town.

Anne cordially asked Francesca how she liked her new job teaching Spanish in the Middle School. Anne's daughter Paige was taking Spanish in 1st grade and absolutely loved it. Anne was *so* proud listening to Paige count to ten—uno, dos, tres, cuatro, cinco, seis, siete, ocho, nueve, diez.

She and Donald thought it just the cutest thing! Anne had been worried that the School Board might not approve the new language teacher for the Elementary School. In a tough budget year, that was quite a controversial hire, and she was relieved when it had been approved.

At 7:50 Madison arrived. She set down the bottle of Columbia Crest she brought and greeted all present. "Has anyone heard from Sarah?" Kathryn told her that she had run into Sarah over the weekend at *Starbucks*, and she had said she was planning to attend. "Maybe her train is running late."

Madison joined Anne, Francesca and Kathryn. Lizbet and Hillary were battling for control of the food situation, so Madison could relax and enjoy her first glass of wine after a particularly draining day in the city. The women asked Madison about her son, Cole, a topic that brought her no end of joy and helped her to focus on something positive. It was actually a blessing that Lizbet was occupied setting out the appetizers; that way she wouldn't grill Madison about what courses and extracurriculars Cole was planning on taking next year. On the other hand, Madison thought it might be fun to needle Lizbet and fib about how she had been told by a close, personal friend on the Admissions Committee that Cole was practically guaranteed early acceptance at Yale. Lizbet was probably calling in every favor she could with anyone even remotely connected to the Admissions Committee. She would ensure that Whitney's application would get the "special" consideration it merited.

A few minutes after Madison's arrival, Carole strode into the room and headed straight for the wine. She poured herself a large glass before joining the others to nibble at the hors d'ouevres. Earlier, just before leaving for the meeting, she and Andrew had had yet another fight over Alexandra's demands. The girls were giving her a hard time as well. They were in a snit because they had to stay at the apartment tonight and it wasn't "fair". Fair? Carole could tell them all about what was fair. Hopefully this meeting would take her mind off her problems, at least for a few hours.

As Giselle glided through the front door at 7:59, the phone started ringing. Kathryn picked up the receiver. She told the others, "Susan has to cancel. Philip still isn't home and she has to stay and help Walker with the dreaded 3D model of the cell that's due next week. She said to say hi to all. She absolutely loved the book."

"Bubble wrap."

All eyes turned to Francesca. "Excuse me?"

"Tell Susan to get some bubble wrap. Bubble wrap works great as the membrane-covered sacs usually filled with water, salts, proteins, carbohydrates and sugars."

Madison asked, "Don't you teach Spanish?"

"I do, but Dr. Coyle has been assigning that project long before even Nicholas entered the seventh grade. I'm not sure what Nicholas learned from the project, but I certainly know my vacuoles."

As everyone laughed, Kathryn told them that Patricia and Margaret couldn't make it tonight—they had e-mailed their regrets. Pat was traveling and Margaret had a Friends of the Library Board meeting. Julia wasn't going to be able to make it either. Kathryn had run into Julia at the Bronxville Women's Club fashion show last week. Julia told Kathryn that she wanted to attend, but there was a Junior League meeting tonight, and Julia absolutely had to show up at that meeting or face the wrath of Eloise Heginbotham. She promised she would see everyone at the June book club discussion. Kathryn didn't know if Sydnie, Quinn, or Chelsea would attend since they hadn't RSVP'd.

Even though Sarah had not yet arrived, it was already 8:20, and…

"Chelsea!" Several of the women turned and spoke at once. "You haven't been to a meeting in so long!" "What on earth have you been up to?"

Hillary hadn't seen Chelsea in a few weeks. She especially wanted to compliment her on the colorful flowers she had planted in the traffic circle outside of Lawrence Hospital. On nice days, Hillary loved to sit outside on nearby benches and eat her salad for lunch. The flowers made the whole area look so lovely. Chelsea cheerfully acknowledged all the greetings, and thanked Hillary, while helping herself to a glass of wine.

It was getting late, and Kathryn tried to usher the women back through the foyer and into the formal living room so they could begin discussing the book. Sarah could always join them when she arrived. Kathryn offered everyone the opportunity to refill their glasses and led the way into the next room.

The ornate, French, 19th-century Gilded Mirror in the cavernous entryway didn't escape Anne's attention. In her expert opinion, Kathryn probably paid $3,300 retail. Hopefully Kathryn would be in the market for one of the pieces Anne had just acquired for the boutique. Anne had a French Baroque Refectory Table she could let Kathryn have for only $24,000. It would look fabulous underneath that mirror. Kathryn certainly had the room for it.

As the women made their way to the living room, Anne paused at the open door to the library on the left. Those built-in mahogany bookcases...and the coffered ceiling...absolutely stunning. Anne knew that the Village trustees had sold a Childe Hassam painting, *Central Park*, for over $4,000,000 to fund the majority of the Bronxville Public Library's renovation. Anne wondered if maybe Kathryn had sold one of her Monet's.

While the others were taking their time chatting and getting settled, Anne's trained eye quickly sized up the expansive formal living room as she carefully walked down the marble steps and paused. Anne mentally ticked off the more noteworthy pieces that caught her attention and "guestimated" what Kathryn and David had probably paid to acquire them.

✓ Mahogany French Empire Recamier Bronze Ormolu—early 19th-century. Anne was sure it cost $15,000, give or take $1,000.

✓ French inlaid secretary abattant. Anne had sold one just like it in her Scarsdale store for $3,000.

✓ Louis XIV Andre Boulle Ormolu Mounted Armoire—at least $135,000, if Kathryn bought it from a reputable dealer.

✓ Pair of 19th-century French Gilt Bergere Chairs—$1,275. The upholstery was in excellent condition.

✓ Antique French Louis XVI Style Coffee Table—$1,500. One of the legs had some minor damage, or Kathryn would have had to pay $2,000 for it.

✓ Late 1700 Gold Leaf French Wedding Mirror—$650. Anne assumed it was a wedding gift. She and Donald had received one just like it for their wedding.

✓ 19th-century French Carved Arm Chair with Original Tapestry— $1,350. The Museum quality condition of the tapestry had probably pushed the price up a bit.

✓ 1893 French Mantle clock by Auguste Moreau—$7,500. Anne couldn't believe the clock was still keeping perfect time.

✓ Ormolu Candelabra—$5,000 for the pair. It was a bit pricey, but the candelabra were quite hard to find.

✓ Pre-19th-century French Brass Sconces in a leaf-and-flower pattern—Anne would appraise them at $900 each.

✓ Palace size Persian Rug—easily $40,000-$50,000.

✓ Marc Chagall's "Le Bouquest Sur Le Toit"—a signed, dated oil and gouache on buff paper. Sotheby's had recently auctioned a similar piece for $90,000-$100,000.

If only Anne had met Kathryn *before* she had furnished her home. Perhaps Kathryn could introduce Anne to some of her neighbors. Surely some of them would be interested in Anne's latest one-of-a-kind finds.

Moving into the center of the room, Anne made a beeline for the chair right next to Lizbet, but she was too late. Lizbet was patting the plump cushion for Giselle to sit next to her. Anne smiled and whispered to Lizbet that she would love for her and Grant, and their friends the Stanfords, to come to a small dinner party she was having next week. Lizbet deftly avoided acknowledging the invitation and instead raised her voice just loud enough for all those nearby to hear. "Has everyone heard that Emma is organizing the sale of a new brochure that she and her neighbors have developed? It is absolutely charming...so many of the historic homes in our village are being showcased as they were originally designed. Everyone must be sure to stop by at the Festival-on-the-Green and purchase a copy." Giselle chimed in with her praise for the brochure. She had seen an advance copy and was so excited that her parent's home was going to be featured. They lived over on Crow's Nest and had just finished a huge renovation effort that restored the structure to its original beauty.

As conversations continued to buzz in all corners of the room, Hillary brought in the food that hadn't been eaten and placed it on the center coffee table. She greeted Giselle warmly and thanked her for her offer of a ride tonight, but then quickly moved away before Giselle could say anything more. Hillary had been uncomfortable with the looks Giselle had been giving her when they were in the kitchen. She probably shouldn't make too much of it—Giselle was likely just jealous of Hillary's weight. Giselle obviously had no self-control, allowing herself to balloon all the way up to 115 pounds.

Madison carried in two more bottles of wine. Francesca and Carole made themselves comfortable on the sofa while Kathryn pulled up one of the Bergere chairs. There was still plenty of room in case those who hadn't responded were able to make it.

As Kathryn called for the group's attention, she heard Sarah coming in the front door. With apologies to all for her tardiness, Sarah quickly found a seat next to Madison. Kathryn paused before going any further so she could get another goblet from the kitchen while Madison uncorked the next bottle of wine.

Madison poured a generous drink for her friend, and as she handed it to her, noted that Sarah looked flushed. If Madison didn't know better, she would have thought that Sarah had already had too much to drink. But Sarah had just arrived directly from her office, so that didn't seem likely. Madison resolved to make a lunch date with Sarah soon, perhaps at Café Centro, since it was located close to both of their offices.

As she settled in her seat, Sarah was bombarded with questions about the recent sexual harassment scandal at JP Morgan that involved two village residents. Unfortunately, the story (and the names of the men) had been reported in all the major newspapers, including the *New York Times.* Try keeping that quiet. Sarah assured everyone that she had no inside information. But Carole wouldn't let it go. She wanted to rehash all the sordid details. Although her words were slightly slurred, every member heard quite clearly the disgust in Sarah's voice when she asked what was the first thing Carole did when she read the names in the papers? "Did you reach for the School Directory to check out where they lived and what grades the children were in?" Frankly, the whole thing made Sarah sick. She knew the families, and she felt awful about what they must be going through. With that "sobering" thought from Sarah, the room quieted.

Sensing her opportunity, Lizbet cleared her throat and gently called for the attention of the group. "Ladies, can we please discuss the book?"

> *"The covers of this book are too far apart."*
>
> *Ambrose Bierce*

Chapter 12

The Book Discussion

*L*izbet was anxious to start the book discussion. She had read this month's selection—*I Don't Know How She Does It: The Life of Kate Reddy, Working Mother*—and was looking forward to sharing her insights on this one. Lizbet knew how Kate did it all right. The Kate Reddy's of the world had people like Lizbet to take care of things so they could selfishly go off to their high-powered careers in the city. These working mothers...always complaining, never pulling their own weight, and constantly relying on others to take care of everything.

Lizbet would be happy to lead the discussion. Of course she would be very careful in how she worded her opinions, her upbringing demanded no less, but these women needed to hear how others viewed their quest to have it all, without the least regard for those around them.

With her right hand held high, and the other firmly on her copy of the book, Lizbet asked for a show of hands of all those who had read this month's selection.

Not one hand went up.

Concealing her irritation quite well she thought, Lizbet smiled and polled each member of the group. Perhaps they hadn't heard the question.

"Madison? As an investment banker and mother, why don't you get things started by sharing your views on how this Kate person, a hedge fund manager, wife, and mother of two young children, manages to have it all."

Madison ventured that, "I probably could relate to Kate Reddy—but I just haven't had time to read the book. It has been such a hectic month at the firm. One of my partners is traveling, my junior associate is on maternity leave, and the School Board meetings have been running so late. And things aren't working out with the new housekeeper I just hired. Does anyone have the name of a good housekeeper you could recommend?"

Maintaining her perfect posture, Lizbet gracefully uncrossed her legs and turned ever so slightly away from Madison.

"Hillary, perhaps you could tell us what you thought of the early scene in the book in which Kate is fraudulently trying to pass off her store bought pies as homemade?"

With expressive hand gestures, Hillary explained that she had been working so many hours at the Hospital these days just trying to keep everything under control, and things at home were just too busy this time of year. "Would anyone like a cranberry muffin? Or some brie? Do you think I should make something different for the June meeting?"

Exasperated, Lizbet repeated the query for Anne.

Anne at least had the grace to blush and mumble something about all the time she had been spending getting ready for the new boutique opening in Bronxville. She started to go off on a tangent about how many hours she had been spending making endless changes to her home renovation plans to satisfy the intransigent demands of the Zoning Board. Just as Lizbet started to interrupt, Anne refocused on the book and asked, "Didn't we say we would read only paperbacks? I'm sure I would have read the book if it were in paperback."

Ever hopeful, Lizbet shifted her attention to Sarah and directed a dazzling smile her way. "Sarah, I'm sure the group would be quite interested in your views on how Celia Harmsworth, the Head of Human Resources at Kate's London firm, EMF, compares to a Human Resources Director at a United States bank such as yours. What do you think are the main similarities and differences between the two cultures?"

Sarah tried to look attentive as she asked Lizbet to please repeat the question. It had been a difficult day at the Bank and Sarah wasn't feeling all that well. She thought it must be the flu or something. Sarah looked around the group and said, "I'm sorry, does someone have a copy of the book I can borrow? It sounds interesting, and I wish I had had an opportunity to read it. Could someone please pass the wine?"

Lizbet took a deep breath. "How about our gracious hostess? Kathryn, what did you think about the character Paula, who supported the family as the children's Nanny?"

Kathryn made no apologies. "I didn't read the book...I haven't even bought the book yet...And don't get me started on nannies."

Lizbet took a sip of her Chardonnay. "Well, now, Carole. Surely you could relate to Candy Stratton's views on parenthood and working mothers as seen from the perspective of someone who has not yet had a child of her own?"

Carole explained how she had gone onto the Westchester Library System's website to reserve the book, but the waiting list was so long, and she just was not going to spend $23.00 for a hardcover book. Carole didn't want to share what she really thought, that she could write the book on being a working mother. True she was a stepparent, and only had the girls every other weekend, but she felt she was somewhat of an expert. Unfortunately, by this point, there was no stopping the oncoming wave of venom. Speaking to no one in particular, she raged, "Andrew's ex-wife Alexandra didn't have to work. Oh, no, not the Alimony Queen. Why should she have to work? She had milked Andrew for everything he had. Perhaps if Alexandra *had* worked, Andrew and I would be living in that stone house on Tanglewylde, and not stuck in my tiny apartment. Perhaps we could discuss divorced mothers who don't work?"

Lizbet quickly turned to Chelsea. "Chelsea, I'm so glad to see that you brought your copy of the book with you. Why don't you comment on how Kate treated her absolutely wonderful husband Richard?"

Chelsea cleared her throat and looked around the beautifully appointed room. "Well, actually, Lizbet, I bought the book last week when I was at the Westchester Mall shopping for some new tennis whites for the boys. *Lord & Taylor* didn't have any completely white shirts left in their sizes, and the Field Club tournament in which they will both be playing is coming up soon, and I meant to read the book, but May is, well, you know. Do you think we could pick a shorter book next month?"

Her energy dissipating, Lizbet scanned the faces for any another member of the group who hadn't spoken. "Giselle? Won't you please tell the other members how you feel about Kate's relationship with her children, poor Emily and Ben?"

Giselle affected a striking pose that had graced many a *Vogue* magazine cover and paused before addressing the group. Although Giselle didn't have that many "blonde moments", when she did, she really did. She looked around the room and made eye contact with each of the women. "Well, when I was in the city last week...I *saw* someone reading it...It looks like a really good book, don't you all think?"

Raising her bejeweled hand, Lizbet politely, but effectively, cut Giselle off before she could utter another word. If Lizbet weren't so well brought up she...

"Ladies..."

Lizbet cleared her throat. "Getting into college—I mean getting *Whitney* into college—is almost a full-time job in itself. And as Memorial Day Committee Chair, I hardly have a moment to myself anymore to get my nails done, or lunch with my girlfriends at Siwanoy, or catch up with my coffee group at *Slave to the Grind*. Please don't misunderstand me. I'm only too glad to give up my personal time to be the Chairperson for such a good cause that benefits the students and faculty, and improves the quality of life in the Bronxville School. And, of course, I recognize that all of you have volunteered in some way to organize an activity, work the children's games, or donate items for the Silent Auction. But I read the book, and I'm certain all of you would agree that no one is busier than I am, isn't that right?"

Turning to the one remaining person who had not yet spoken, Lizbet expressed her sincere hope that surely Francesca had read this month's selection.

In a soft, melodic voice, Francesca acknowledged that she had indeed read the book.

With a collective sigh, everyone in the group gratefully directed their undivided attention to Francesca.

Perhaps Francesca was empowered by her natural empathy for the overwhelmed women in the room who had not had an opportunity to read the book—although it also could be attributed to the quantity of wine she had consumed over the past hour. Or maybe it was a belated thank you to all those working women who had cheerfully volunteered for every unglamorous committee when Francesca was Elementary School Council Chair. (Who wanted to call 20 sleeping families at 6:00 in the morning to announce an emergency school closing?) Whatever the reason, Francesca rose to the challenge, both literally and figuratively, and took control of the floor from Lizbet.

Using the same flair for the dramatic that she brought to her classroom each day, Francesca proceeded, with dead-on accuracy, to bring to life many of the characters featured in the life of Kate Reddy. Transforming her voice to capture the essence of each of them, Francesca quoted key passages from the novel. She eloquently evoked the feelings of the harried Kate…the longings of Kate's husband Richard with his gift of the Agent Provocateur bra…and the frustrations of Kate's female colleagues as a result of unprofessional slights by their irascible boss, Rod Task, and venture capitalist co-worker, Chris Bunce.

Referencing several hilarious as well as poignant excerpts, Francesca made the group feel the lure of temptation offered by Kate's American client, Jack Abelhammer…the cruel manipulations perpetrated by Emily and Ben's Nanny, Paula…and last, but certainly not least, the sting of the judgments meted out by the "Muffia", that powerful clique of stay-at-home mothers who ran her children's school.

Thinking about the characters that comprised the Muffia, Francesca wanted to finish with a question that she felt would resonate with many of the women in the room. Turning to the appropriate page, she described for the group the incident in which Kate was "blanked" by one of her clients. She waited a beat. "Surely no one here has ever been *blanked* by someone in our own town?"

Several women shouted out some familiar names, including that of Jayne Branson. Chelsea raised her voice so she could be heard above the din. "For heaven's sake, Ted coaches the soccer team of Jayne's son, Fredrick…We've been chaperones together on at least three of the same class trips…I sat next to her at the Community Fund dinner last year…

And *still* she acts as if we've never met. I absolutely refuse to introduce myself to her one more time!"

Sarah lamented that several of the career "ladies-who-lunch" had *blanked* her on more than one occasion. They way some of them picked their power tables at the country club and jockeyed for position, one would think they were strategizing how to pass a revolutionary tax reform program that would stimulate GDP without negatively impacting the long-term budget deficit.

Francesca had obviously hit a familiar chord. With everyone starting to talk at once, she collapsed in a heap on the sofa and accepted a tall glass of ice water from Hillary. With a tight-lipped smile, Lizbet politely joined her fellow book club members as they enthusiastically rewarded Francesca's superb performance with a standing ovation. After waiting what she deemed a respectable interval for the applause to subside, Lizbet endeavored to recapture everyone's attention.

"Excuse me…Ladies?"

"Ladies?"

"*Always do sober what you said you'd do drunk. That will teach you to keep your mouth shut.*"

Ernest Hemingway

Chapter 13

The Meeting Concludes

Before Lizbet could utter another word, Hillary rose and said her goodbyes to the group. "G'night everybody. It was great seeing all of you again. I really wish I could stay later, but I have so much to do before I go to bed tonight." She asked Lizbet to please send her the notice for the next meeting. "Thanks for keeping us so organized, Lizbet. I'll see you Memorial Day weekend!"

Anne quickly followed suit and asked Hillary if she could give her a lift to the Avalon apartments over by the train station where she and Donald were renting. She explained that her Beemer was in the shop and they hadn't ransomed it yet. Donald had dropped her off earlier after stopping by Prescott Avenue to check the progress on their home, but he was probably putting Paige to bed, and she didn't want to disturb him. Anne spoke in a low voice to Hillary. "Of course, Nanny Nonny normally puts Paige to bed, but until our house is ready, we are forced to rent an apartment for Nanny in Mt. Vernon, and she can't fully perform her duties. It is all too, too horrible, don't you think?" Hillary just smiled noncommittally, and with many thanks to Kathryn, the two women headed for Hillary's Range Rover.

Giselle was disappointed that Hillary was leaving so soon. She had hoped to catch Hillary alone for a private chat, but Hillary clearly did not want to be "caught." Maybe they would run into each other at the Memorial Day Bake Sale when they worked their assigned shifts…or at the *Run for Fun*, since Hillary would undoubtedly enter the 5K race, although not for "fun."

Before Kathryn could close the front door behind Anne and Hillary, Francesca picked up her bag and yawned. "Sorry, but I really need to get going too. It was an especially fun meeting tonight. Thanks for hosting Kathryn..." As Francesca moved towards the door, she turned to Lizbet. "Please keep me posted on the next meeting. I promise I'll have a meeting at my house in the Fall, but please, *not* before Back to School Night. Why don't you put me down for November?"

Chelsea checked her watch and decided it was probably an opportune time for her to make her exit as well. She was expecting an early delivery Friday morning—the white, carmine and violet Rhododendron shrubs for the Colonial she was landscaping over on Homesdale. If Chelsea had any energy left when she got home, she probably should also put the finishing touches on her proposal for the new home on Summit.

Giselle asked Chelsea if she could hitch a ride with her. While Giselle felt safe walking in the village at night, she wanted a chance to talk to Chelsea to find out how her boys were doing. They were such great kids, and Giselle missed seeing them in the neighborhood. As they got older, the boys had been given increasing privileges that included being able to walk into town with friends, or ride their bikes further and further away from their small private street. Giselle and Chelsea lived only a few houses away from each other, but they never seemed to have any time to talk anymore. These days Giselle felt as if her friendships were being determined more and more by which children were in the classes of Lily and Hannah. It was just easier to socialize with the mothers of her children's friends. Giselle could barely keep up with her Lily and Hannah's play dates, never mind set up "play dates" of her own.

After murmuring farewells to the departing women, Madison and Sarah refilled their glasses and settled back in their chairs. Reaching into her leather tote, Madison pulled her Palm Pilot from its case. "No excuses, Sarah. Let's pick a date for lunch next week. A *long* lunch. We really need to talk. How does Friday look for you?"

Carole felt a bit left out. Didn't anyone want to talk about what she wanted to talk about? She just didn't get these women. At least she could tell Andrew that she had tried, but she just didn't fit in with this group.

Especially Sarah. Sarah was so touchy, jumping down Carole's throat simply because she had asked about the latest gossip. Carole couldn't put her finger on exactly why she didn't click with these women, but...With startling clarity, Carole suddenly realized the real reason these women didn't warm up to her. Many of these women were probably good friends of Andrew's ex-wife, Alexandra. Of course...That must be it! With a good-night to the remaining members of the book club, Carole politely thanked the hostess and walked to her car alone. She unlocked her ten-year-old Camry and slid into the front seat. Hopefully Andrew's girls would be in the guest room with the door closed by the time Carole got back to the apartment so she could avoid another confrontation. Although this had not been one of her better days, it could still be saved. She vowed to make up with Andrew when she got home.

Always the perfect guest, Lizbet smiled sweetly and began to collect the empty wineglasses and plates to help Kathryn with the clean-up. Poor Kathryn. After all, she no longer had live-in household help. It must be too terrible for her. She and Grant would have to have Kathryn over for dinner soon. Maybe she would even introduce Kathryn to one of her friends who was considering buying in Bronxville. Kathryn could probably use the commission.

Before removing the trays from the coffee table, Lizbet offered Sarah and Madison something to eat, but they declined. They certainly seemed deep in conversation, but not about next month's book selection. Lizbet could have sworn she heard them say something about the Bronxville School Muffia. She must have misheard them, since she and her friends could never be accused of being like those caricatures of stay-at-home mothers in the book—the ones who get an A+ in micromanaging their children's lives...who have their children's teachers' numbers on speed dial...and bake those perfect tortes for the Memorial Day Bake Sale. None of her friends were like that.

Lizbet joined Kathryn in the great room to help put away the food—so much left-over food!—and collect the empty wine bottles. My goodness, thought Lizbet, Kathryn would need a larger recycling bin to hold all of these bottles for the Wednesday pickup. Imagine what the sanitation workers were going to think. Lizbet shuddered. Thankfully it was Kathryn's house and not hers. Lizbet was always so careful about her recycling. It was a reflection of her home and family, and she would never want to give the neighbors, or those nice sanitation men, anything to gossip about. Certainly not about her home.

With everything in its rightful place, Lizbet said her goodbyes to Madison, Sarah and Kathryn and reminded them not to forget their Memorial Day assignments for next week. "Pray for good weather! See you soon. Bye for now!"

With only Madison and Sarah remaining, Kathryn pulled up a chair and poured herself and her guests another glass of wine.

It was only then that they realized they hadn't picked a book for next month's meeting. They burst out laughing and raised their glasses in a toast. "Here's to the Bronxville Book Club…Maybe one of these days we'll actually have time to read the book!"

"*I am a marvelous housekeeper. Every time I leave a man I keep his house.*"

Zsa Zsa Gabor

Chapter 14

Kathryn

brokerbabe@bxvillerealestate.com

athryn thought they would never leave! At least Lizbet had helped with the clean up, so it shouldn't take too long before Kathryn was ready to head upstairs to get set for tomorrow. At times like this, she really missed her former household staff headed by the highly capable Mrs. Crawford. Maybe someday Kathryn could hire them back (except for the Nanny from hell, Anjolie, of course!), if she continued to do well selling homes in the village.

She just needed to remember to practice her affirmation statements. As a hostess gift for a party she gave for her bridge club, Kathryn had received a basket of goodies from some new-age boutique in Greenwich Village. The basket contained beautifully-illustrated bookmarks with different affirmation statements printed on each. Kathryn really got turned on to the idea that women had the power to change their lives by saying, thinking, or feeling something positive every day. As she put away the last of the unused crystal goblets, Kathryn repeated her personal favorites:

❖ *I am a magnet for abundance in the form of wealth, health and happiness.*

❖ *I take my time and rest, relax and rejuvenate.*

❖ *I let go of things that are no longer useful.*

❖ *I create relationships that are fair and pleasurable.*

❖ *I invent creative solutions to the challenges in my life.*

❖ *I am attractive because I feel good about myself.*

Satisfied that everything was back in its rightful place, Kathryn turned off the downstairs lights and slowly made her way up the back stairs to her office. With a few clicks on her Dell, she opened AOL and checked her e-mail. Scanning the messages, she skipped the spam mail and selected the message from Joan. Yes! The closing was all set for tomorrow. Kathryn just needed to stop by the office for some notarized papers before heading up to the closing in White Plains. Kathryn turned off the computer and continued down the hall to check on Pryce.

Pryce was seated squarely in front of the television in his bedroom playing *Grand Theft Auto: Vice City.* (Wasn't that game banned in Australia?) No wonder he hadn't made a peep all night. Why couldn't someone find a way to put children's schoolwork on a PlayStation 2 disk? Kathryn gave Pryce his two-minute warning before lights out. "Brush your teeth and hop into bed. Early day tomorrow!" With a kiss and a hug, Kathryn said good night and quietly closed his door.

Alone in her master bedroom suite, Kathryn padded across the thick cream-colored carpeting and stepped into the bathroom. She placed a fluffy, oversized towel on the stool by the double-ended, roll-top Casteron bath with cast-iron feet. She just loved the new Christo Lefroy Brooks tub and fixtures from his 2003 turn-of-the-century (was that an oxymoron?) French line. She lit some votive candles, turned up the volume on the Andrea Bocelli CD that Pryce had given her last Christmas, and drew a hot bath.

Kathryn couldn't wait to try this new body soak her friend Allison had given her for her birthday—*Kisses by Candlelight.* She began to read the description on the back of the bottle while undressing:

"Kisses by Candlelight effacera le stress du quotidien et ravivera vos plus chers souvenirs, rappelant à votre mémoire les moments les plus

heureux de votre vie. Son parfum romantique et soyeux vous apportera joie et sérénité. Le parfum onctueux de Kisses by Candlelight vous fait revivre les plus beaux instants de votre vie, ceux qui apaisent et réjouissent votre vie, ceux qui apaisent et rejouissent votre âme."

Her French was rustier than she thought. She cheated and read the English translation:

"Escape from the everyday pressures of life, and reconnect with cherished memories that bring comfort and pleasure. Let the rich, romantic blend of Kisses by Candlelight help you recapture the solace that comes only with thoughts of your favorite things. Allow the decadent, creamy scent to carry you back to those moments that soothe and comfort your soul."

Kathryn carefully stepped into the tub and thought about her life. She really was very fortunate after all. She had Pryce, her health, a career she loved, and good friends. With each passing day, David was becoming as distant a memory as her fluent French. Maybe in the future there would be a new man in her life, but for now, Kathryn could take care of herself and Pryce just fine. Pryce did need a little more attention, though, and preferably of the male variety.

As she relaxed her body and her mind, Kathryn suddenly had a wickedly brilliant idea. Her friend Chloe, whose son Chaz was in the fourth grade with Pryce, had a Nanny for her daughter, Margeaux, and a *Manny* for Chaz. Tomorrow Kathryn would call the New England School of Nannies to get a list of their male graduates—or Mannies, as they liked to be called—that would be available for part-time employment in southern Westchester. Pryce would be thrilled. And best of all, Kathryn would find a way to send the bill for their new, and preferably gorgeous, Manny to David!

Looking back on the evening, Kathryn had to admit that all things considered, the meeting actually went quite smoothly. Her cleaning woman had shown up—thank God, since no room on the first floor was safe from Anne's laser vision. The hors d'ouevres were delicious—Hillary certainly liked to bake. And Kathryn hadn't run out of wine (just barely). Anne and Lizbet didn't make a scene, so that was a plus. Lizbet got as good as she gave, but you had to give the devil her due—she did use her special "talents" to benefit the school treasury. And Francesca's rendition of the main characters in the book was hysterical. Given all that had happened in her personal life, Kathryn could sympathize with the characters on both sides of the fence in the whole working mother debate. But as God was her witness, she would never be accused of being a member of the Muffia. Even if she wanted to, Kathryn just didn't have the time or the inclination.

It had been such a good meeting that Kathryn decided she might even purchase, *and read*, a copy of the book they had "discussed" tonight. She wondered what book they were going to read for next month. Her last thought before submerging herself in the bubbles was not to worry, Lizbet would be sure to let her know all the details.

> *"It is the wretchedness of being rich that you have to live with rich people."*
>
> Logan Pearsall Smith

Chapter 15

Anne

arichardson@annetiques.com

With a wave to Hillary, Anne pushed open the doors to the front entrance of the Avalon and entered the unoccupied elevator car in the center of the lobby. The Avalon apartments certainly were super convenient for Donald's commute into Grand Central, but Anne couldn't wait until their house on Prescott was finished and they could all finally move in, including Nanny Nonny. She missed having Nanny close at hand, but what could they do?

She leaned back in the elevator and closed her eyes—and just as suddenly opened them with a start. Oh God, she had promised Paige she would buy some crepe paper so Paige could decorate her bike for the Memorial Day parade. Anne would have to remember to stop by CVS before heading over to the boutique in the morning. Although obviously stretched too thin—speaking of thin, would someone please give Hillary a decent meal!—Anne needed to get better organized. With all that she had going on these days, she was forgetting more than she was remembering.

As the doors opened on the second floor, Anne slowly stepped out and turned left to Apartment 2D. Easing her key into the lock, she quietly stepped inside and tiptoed into the den. She put down her purse and collapsed in a chair. Although she was bone tired, she was glad she had been able to make the meeting tonight. Kathryn's house was every bit as incredible as Anne had imagined it would be. If there were more Kathryn's in this town, Anne's business would take off in no time. She must remember to invite Kathryn for lunch at *Pan e Vino* next week so they could explore future business opportunities. After all, Kathryn was in a perfect position to have seen the inside of most of the houses in Bronxville, either from when she was married to David, or from when she had shown them to prospective buyers. Kathryn could introduce Anne to potential clients who would benefit from the boutique's finest pieces. And in return, Anne could steer some of her clients from her other stores to Kathryn, in case they were looking to make the move to Bronxville or one of the comparable surrounding communities.

She stared at all the papers on her antique secretary that needed to be signed before final approval would be issued for the grand opening of *Annetiques*. At least the boutique opening was on schedule. Anne wished she could say the same for her house. McMansion indeed. When she had lunch with Kathryn she would have to enlist her support in getting the renovations approved. Higher property values would mean higher commissions for Kathryn. Surely Kathryn would agree that Anne's newer, grander home would only enhance the neighborhood.

Maybe Giselle could become any ally, too. Giselle had lived in Bronxville all her life—she must have some friends on Prescott. Giselle might not be all that bright, but more importantly, she did have the right connections *and* a good address on Governors Road. Anne resolved to call Giselle in the morning to set up a play date for their daughters. Paige and Lily were about the same age. Anne would make sure that the girls became the best of friends.

Anne wondered what was up with Lizbet. For some reason, Anne couldn't seem to get a quiet word with Lizbet...or Chelsea either. Good thing Anne wasn't paranoid, or she might have thought some of the book club members were actually avoiding her!

Carole wasn't avoiding her, but Anne decided not to pursue any further relationship with her outside the monthly meetings. Carole really couldn't be of too much assistance—she so clearly did not fit in this town. Maybe Anne should get to know Andrew's ex-wife Alexandra instead—didn't she live near Prescott, on Sunset & Paradise, in that gorgeous Victorian?

Racking her sleep-deprived brain, Anne tried to think of whom else in the book club she might be able to rally to her cause. Francesca wasn't likely to be much help. Anne thought she overheard Francesca say something about how her husband's business wasn't doing very well. What was his name? Richard? Roger? No, Roger was Sarah's husband. Was it Randall? Whatever. And what did Francesca say her husband did? Was he a book publisher? Since Francesca was a part-timer at the school, her job probably didn't pay very much, but it would put her in touch with a lot of the right parents. The parents probably liked Francesca's teaching style— she was definitely entertaining at the meeting tonight. Poor, but entertaining.

Sarah and Madison might prove useful in furthering Anne's cause. Perhaps Anne should invite both of them to the grand opening of her boutique. They seemed to be good friends, and it would be wise for Anne to get to know them better. As a School Board Trustee, Madison knew everything that was going on in this town. Sarah's husband Roger might be a good resource, too. Anne was always reading about his latest tennis triumphs over a lot of the movers and shakers at the Club. Anne decided she would call Madison and Sarah in the morning to set up a brunch date at *Scarborough Fair*, a positively charming restaurant tucked on a side street off Pondfield Road.

Reluctantly, Anne heaved herself out of the chair and picked up the stack of mail on the dining room table that Donald had sorted. The latest *Review Press* was on top. Anne didn't have the energy to read one more article about the school construction delays or budget woes. Nor did she have the stomach to peek inside to see if there were any more letters to the editor about her "McMansion."

Thumbing through the pile, she set aside several bills and opened up the June booklet for the Field Club. The Tapas and Margarita Night sounded like great fun—maybe she and Donald should sign up. There was a reminder that swim team practices would begin in early June. Anne needed to put those dates on Paige's calendar—June was already quite full. The spring junior tennis program would end on June 13, but then the summer tennis lessons would begin on June 20. Paige would be graduating from the Davis Cuppers to the Grand Slammers!

Anne's eye was drawn to a large, pastel-colored envelope decorated with an array of baby animals. Breaking the seal, Anne saw that inside was an engraved invitation for Paige. Beneath the chiffon pink ribbon affixed to the cream colored card were the details of a party.

> *Pony and Petting Zoo Party*
>
> *In honor of*
>
> *Kyle's 7th Birthday!*
>
> *Saturday, June 14*
>
> *2:00–5:00 p.m.*
>
> *788 Elm Rock Road*
>
> *Bronxville, New York*
>
> *Regrets only*

Even though the invitation said "Regrets Only", Anne would RSVP anyway and offer to stay at the house during the party—to help, of course. The large, old houses on Elm Rock were absolutely spectacular, and she couldn't wait to get inside one of them.

Mindy, the class mother for Paige's first grade class, had mailed a notice of the class picnic and pool party planned for June 17 at the Cahill's house on Beechwood. Anne would have to make sure that she was the one who dropped Paige off at the picnic so she could get a good look at the backyard. How could the Cahill's have a pool back there? They must know someone on the Zoning Board.

Before the class party on the 17th, Anne would have to wrap that antique inkwell she had picked on a recent shopping trip to England.

Anne had already contributed to the class gift for the teacher, but the inkwell would make a perfect extra thank-you to Mrs. McDonald for taking such good care of Paige in first grade. Especially since the Bronxville School kept the children together with the same teacher for the first and second grades, it couldn't hurt for Mrs. McDonald to have a special remembrance of Paige.

Near the bottom of the pile of mail was a flier from the Twin Lake Stables. Anne knew she had better get Paige enrolled in their summer camp riding program before it reached capacity. Paige's schedule was filling up so quickly! (Maybe Anne should get Paige her own Personal Digital Assistant as a little gift to celebrate the end of 1st grade.) Anne would definitely have to find the time to fit the riding lessons in somehow. Paige just loved horses and Anne wouldn't want her to be disappointed.

Anne almost missed the postcard from Mimi Clayborne inviting her to preview the fall line of suede clothing that Mimi sold from her Bronxville home. Engraved over a background graphic of several hangers in shades of brown, orange, gold, and green, were the details of the sale:

What:	**Suede Sensations!** **Fall Preview**
When:	**June 8 & 9** **9:00 a.m. to 2:00 p.m.**
Where:	**1977 Midland Avenue** **Bronxville, New York**

Anne had heard about these events from her friend Madeleine, but she had never been to one. Perhaps it would be good way to meet other women in the town who might become valued clients of her new boutique. At least that way she could justify to Donald why she would need to spend $750 on an ultra-suede blazer that she would be buying off a rack in someone's living room.

As she placed the mail back on the table and turned to leave the dining room, Anne noticed a *Party Tyme* bag on the sideboard. Opening the bag she saw three large rolls of red, white, and blue crepe paper with tiny silver stars. With all the stress she was under, Donald must have known she would forget. He probably had asked his secretary to pick these up. He was so thoughtful.

With a deep sigh, Anne locked up the apartment and joined Donald in the back bedroom where he was reviewing the latest concessions in the design of their "dream" home. "Nightmare" was becoming a more apt description of their home. Anne was tired, but seeing Donald's disgusted expression gave her a sudden jolt of adrenaline.

"Damn these people. Damn, damn, damn! Just who appointed them the ultimate arbiters of good taste? I am so sick of their superior, know-it-all attitudes, and narrow-minded thinking. Well, Donald, we will show them. What is it my good friend Bailey always says? Don't get mad…get even."

Anne made a silent vow. If she had to spend every dollar Donald had, she would give these people a run for their considerable money…or kill herself trying.

"You have to stay in shape. My grandmother, she started walking five miles a day when she was 60. She's 97 today and we don't know where the hell she is."

Ellen DeGeneres

Chapter 16

Hillary

never2thin@fitness.org.com

fter dropping Anne off at the Avalon, Hillary pulled her SUV into her driveway with the Belgian Block apron and edging that Bradford had just installed. Although Hillary hadn't been in favor of such an unnecessary expense—the old driveway had been in excellent condition—she had to admit that it did look much nicer. Making sure her Range Rover wasn't too close to Bradford's Jaguar, Hillary turned off the ignition and hopped down from the driver's seat. She hated how Brad always made fun of her when she drove the SUV. "Such a big car for such a tiny person, Hillary. Can you even see over the dashboard?" Well, he could have his Jag. She wouldn't trade cars with him for anything. This car made her feel so much more in control.

Walking around to the front of their English cottage, Hillary noticed that all the lights in the upstairs bedrooms were off. Brad must have put Tyler to bed and turned in early himself. No need to hurry inside on such an unseasonably warm night.

Hillary paused by her brilliant pink azaleas and light blue hydrangeas before settling into the white-wicker chair on the front porch. Rocking back and forth, she stared at the pots of deep violet and blue pansies gently moving in the evening breeze. She felt her body and her mind slowly releasing the stresses of the day.

It was so peaceful on Hobart Street. During the day, this family neighborhood was teeming with children, but now the only sound she heard was some faraway music drifting over from the Concordia College dorms.

Although some of the older residents on the block occasionally complained about the noise from the college kids, Hillary actually enjoyed their proximity and thought they made terrific neighbors.

Brad and Hillary's own college years seemed so long ago. Those were the days. Back then it had been so easy for Hillary to lose a quick five pounds if she wanted to before a party or special date. Now she had to work so hard to keep herself trim. Not that Bradford seemed to appreciate all her efforts. You would think he'd be happy she weighed even less than she did when they got married. Men had it so much easier. Ever since she had known him, Bradford had always seemed to be able to eat whatever he wanted and not gain an ounce. When Hillary got pregnant with Ty, she had gained almost 18 pounds! Her mother had the nerve to tell her that it was a miracle she had even been able to get pregnant, given all the problems she had had with her period over the years. But her mother needn't have worried. After that experience, Hillary made a vow that she'd never get pregnant (or fat) again.

With a sigh, Hillary forced her mind back to the present, and thought about more pleasant things. Tonight's gathering had been fun. It had definitely taken her mind off her woes, at least for a few hours. The other women really seemed to enjoy the muffins and double-fudge brownies she had baked. Hillary would make something similar for the June meeting… maybe oatmeal raisin muffins instead of cranberry, and a nice carrot cake.

There certainly had been plenty to drink at Kathryn's house. Hillary would have tried the Chardonnay, but 4 ounces would have cost her 90 calories! How could the other women waste all those calories? The sparkling water Kathryn served was so delicious, and a much better alternative. It tasted especially refreshing with a large slice of lemon. Perhaps at the next meeting Hillary would try her mineral water with a slice of lime instead, just for variety.

The only sour note of the evening had been those strange looks from Giselle. What was her problem? At 5 feet 11 inches, Giselle probably felt so overweight at 115 pounds and envied how Hillary kept herself in such good shape. Massimo was such a handsome man. In the fashion business he must meet a lot of tall, thin, attractive models. Giselle had better watch her weight, or…

Hillary was lost in her reverie when her cat Hester appeared from behind the Mercedes station wagon in her neighbor's yard and meowed to get into the house for the night. Once she figured out that Hillary was not going to get up to let her in, Hester jumped up into her lap and curled up into a ball. Hillary stroked the cat's fur and thought about what she would do tomorrow.

If she got up earlier than usual, she could do her at-home workout and still have time to sneak into the exercise room in the Physical Therapy unit before the first patients arrived. The staff really wasn't supposed to be in there, but it was shame to let all that equipment go unused. After a quick change, she could bury herself under a mountain of paperwork and avoid Dr. Westland at all costs. If she put her phone on forward and worked in the patient records' room all morning, maybe she wouldn't be found at all. For lunch she could walk over to the duck pond with her mixed salad of Iceberg and Romaine lettuce (with an extra-large lemon wedge) that she'd bring from home. This way she wouldn't even have to go to the cafeteria where she might run into the good doctor. In the afternoon she had a meeting in one of the hospital annexes, and Westland never went near those buildings, so there was no chance of running into him there.

It could work.

Reluctantly, Hillary got up and unlocked the side door. Letting Hester in ahead of her, she stepped into the mudroom and activated the home alarm system for the night. Walking softly through the rambling downstairs rooms, Hillary sensed that everything was under control.

Returning to the gourmet kitchen, Hillary perused the built-in cabinet shelves containing every imaginable type of cookbook that she had accumulated over the years. While she and Lizbet had been helping Kathryn tonight, Lizbet had told Hillary how she wanted this to be the best Memorial Day bake sale *ever.* Hillary would be only too happy to do her part to contribute to its success! She needed to find just the right dessert. Thumbing through the well-worn books, Hillary chose a recipe for a red, white and blueberry pie—a flaky pie crust filled with all kinds of delicious ingredients, including white baking chocolate, strawberries, cream cheese, vanilla, and fresh blueberries. Maybe she should also make a white angel food cake with coconut frosting…and a raspberry tart…and perhaps two dozen butter cookies decorated with red, white and blue sugar. Hillary couldn't wait to get started baking for the event.

Still very much awake, Hillary decided she would watch CNN in the basement so she wouldn't disturb her sleeping family. She might as well change into her sweatpants and baggy T-shirt (Boys Size "Medium") and use the treadmill downstairs while she watched the news. Just thinking about all that food made her feel *so* fat. She needed to work off those extra calories.

After all, as Hillary always said, "One could never be too rich or too thin, could one?"

> "All mothers are working mothers."
>
> Unknown

Chapter 17

Francesca

maestramama@westchesterteachers.edu

obert was waiting on the front porch of their townhouse. He patted the bench and invited Francesca to sit with him and enjoy the magnificent nighttime sky.

Putting his arm around Francesca, Robert asked how the book club meeting went. When Francesca started to tell him that she was sorry, but she hadn't been able to get Sarah alone to ask if she would introduce him to some of her colleagues at JP Morgan, Robert put his hand up to cut short her apologies. He didn't want to talk about his work. Not tonight. He knew he had been sounding very discouraged lately. In fact, there was something else he wanted to tell her…something Nicholas had told him.

Francesca stiffened.

In a serious voice, Robert began.

"Reaching the end of a job interview, the Human Resources Director asked the hotshot young Engineer, fresh out of MIT, 'And what starting salary were you looking for?'

The engineer coolly said, 'In the neighborhood of $125,000 a year, depending on the benefits package.'

The interviewer said, 'Well, what would you say to a package of 5 weeks vacation, 14 paid holidays, full medical and dental, company-matching retirement fund to 50% of salary, and a company car leased every 2 years—for starters, say a red Corvette?'

The engineer tried to control his excitement, but sat straight up and said, 'Wow! Are you kidding?'

'Yeah,' the interviewer shrugged, 'But you started it.'"

Francesca laughed until she cried. "Where did you hear that?"

"Nicholas got it off the Internet…you know, that thing my old college classmate Al Gore invented?"

Francesca was still laughing when their next door neighbor Gregory opened his door, smiled a hello, and set off towards Meadow Avenue to walk his Bichon Frise, Belle. Robert and Francesca remembered when Nicholas used to take care of Belle whenever Gregory was on vacation or working late in the city. Where had the time gone?

Robert shifted the discussion to their son's latest news. Nicholas was busy completing his application to study abroad next year. Francesca knew that somehow they would find a way for him to take advantage of such a spectacular opportunity. As Robert's grandmother used to joke, "Where there's a will, there are relatives." And speaking of relatives, to save money, maybe Nicholas could study in London and board with Robert's cousin Edward. Wasn't Edward always telling them he had plenty of room in his bachelor flat; his door was always open. He would be delighted to have Nicholas stay with him for a semester. Although Francesca had always hoped that Nicolas would go to Spain or Italy and brush up on his language skills, she knew that no matter where he went, it would be the experience of a lifetime.

To cover the extra expenses a trip abroad would entail, Francesca and Robert talked about ways of cutting back on some of the monthly expenses that they could control. They had been putting it off, but it was probably time for them to refinance their mortgage. Rates were at all time historical lows. Madison had been advising Francesca to get rid of their 8% mortgage and get one of the new ones in the 5% range. They had been waiting for the right time, but how much lower could rates possibly fall? A refinance on their original loan would significantly lower their monthly bills. They also didn't have to lease the new Volvo they had their eye on. The old Volvo they had bought used, when they were teaching Nicholas to drive, wouldn't exactly turn heads in this town, but it got them where they needed to go, and best of all, there was no monthly payment!

Looking ahead, with any luck, Francesca would be able to work more hours when the new school year began in September. Depending on how many children moved in or out of the district, and how many of the faculty returned, there were always last minute changes that might work in her favor. Maybe, like Chelsea, Francesca could teach a course at the Bronxville Adult School at night. They offered several programs in conversational Spanish that Francesca would enjoy teaching, and the extra money could at least pay for Nicholas' textbooks. If she really wanted to, Francesca knew she could probably start a private language tutoring service for children in the Elementary School. Parents like Anne and Donald Richardson would certainly want their children to take individual lessons to supplement the school program. But that could quickly get out of hand, as Francesca had seen all too often. With mothers like Anne and Lizbet in the community, it wouldn't surprise Francesca if she were asked to chaperone a trip to Spain as an Elementary School enrichment program!

Robert reminded Francesca that things had a way of working out. They both just needed to stay positive. Francesca told him that maybe Kathryn could teach her about that whole affirmation thing she practiced. It definitely seemed to be working for her. Francesca tried to sound serious as she intoned, "I have faith in the future I cannot see."

It was getting late…Robert needed to get up early the next morning to catch the 7:14 Express for a breakfast meeting with a potential client that sounded promising. The owners of this company were expanding their franchise all along the northeastern corridor. They had been wildly successful in the Southern states, providing expanded in-home health services to the elderly that enabled them to remain in their own homes for as long as possible. At least it wasn't another dot-com or anything even remotely connected with financial services.

Given her "commute," Francesca could afford to sleep in a bit longer in the morning, but the 8:00 a.m. school bell would be ringing before she knew it. Reluctantly, Francesca rose from the bench, led the way through the front door, and turned off the porch light. It would be difficult, but she had faith that somehow she and Robert would manage.

"I have faith in the future I cannot see."

"Que sera, sera."

"I'm tired of all this nonsense about beauty being only skin-deep. That's deep enough. What do you want, an adorable pancreas?"

Jean Kerr

Chapter 18

Giselle

modelcitizen@thelingerielady.com

Giselle waved goodbye to Chelsea and watched as she pulled the Jeep into her own driveway at the end of Governors Road. Stepping into the hushed entryway of her large Colonial, Giselle paused at the foot of the spiral staircase. She could hear Massimo's muffled voice upstairs as he read Hannah a bedtime story. It sounded like one of those Lemony Snicket books—*The Carnivorous Carnival?* It wouldn't be Giselle's first choice as an appropriate bedtime story (those poor Baudelaire orphans and the series of unfortunate events they were forced to endure!), but at least Massimo was reading to Hannah, and she clearly wasn't complaining.

Giselle knew she should turn in early, but she was still wide-awake and suddenly bursting with ideas for her next signature collection. She and her partners had just signed a contract for a large booth at next year's Intimate Apparel Salon in Manhattan. She had to come up with some killer items to top the purple lace nursing bras and funky, flannel bed jackets their competition had displayed at this year's show. As payback for all her years modeling the often incredibly uncomfortable pieces created by men (just who invented the thong?), Giselle wanted to design male body shapers and market them as the ultimate undergarment for the macho man. But she would bide her time until just the right opportunity to pull off that coup.

For now, Giselle would draw on the evening's events and the women in her book club for inspiration. Ideas she had been mulling over for the past few weeks started to come into sharper focus—Giselle would produce an amazing new lingerie and sleepwear line for the full spectrum of women who were somewhere between maternity and menopause!

Rushing into her home office to jot down ideas and rough sketches before she could forget, and before the alcohol wore off, Giselle grabbed an oversized spiral notebook and a sharp #2 pencil from the Chippendale Ladies Writing Table. Armed with the necessary supplies, she moved over to the window and sank into a comfy, deep-cushioned Manhasset chaise in butter yellow. Stretching out and crossing her long, tan legs, Giselle opened the sketchbook and began to scribble furiously.

She would begin with something for the hostess of tonight's meeting, Kathryn. For women with Kathryn's impeccable taste who had recently re-entered the dating scene, Giselle would design an elegant silk charmeuse full-length gown with a plunging back—lower than any they had done last year—and whisper-thin spaghetti straps. Color: Black only.

Giselle turned to a clean page and thought about the inimitable Lizbet. Petite women like Lizbet would snap up a satin tunic top—ballet neck and side slits—paired with gently draping pants with a fitted waist. One color would never be enough for these ladies who would want to coordinate their sleepwear with their bedding. The outfit would have to be offered in a wide variety of colors, including French pink, purple ice, cornflower blue, coral rose, pale jonquil, periwinkle, pearl gray, mint green, rhubarb, sea green, hibiscus…

Anne had Giselle stumped for a minute until she remembered about *Annetiques*. Women like Anne would appreciate an off-white, vintage-inspired cotton gown with eyelet lace and satin trim. The gowns would have to be offered as one-of-a kind pieces with limited distribution so as to maintain their value. Perhaps a mother/daughter line would work if Giselle designed coordinating cotton nightgowns for girls, sizes 7 through 14. Maybe even a mother, daughter, and *doll* line of matching gowns would be a hit. Anne would be her best customer.

Flipping to another page in her notebook, Giselle turned her thoughts to a new collection for women like Carole—wasn't she trying to get pregnant? A thin rayon and silk slip in sapphire blue, with a matching reversible kimono—in sapphire blue and pearl white—would look very sexy. Giselle had better make sure to offer it in hot pink as well…and fire engine red. Maybe she should also create a line of sheer marquisette corsets with just a hint of lace, and special touches like clean, barely visible seams.

It was easy to come up with new takes on classic designs for natural beauties like Francesca. Giselle could visualize Francesca modeling a mid-calf-length silk shift in pale wisteria, cut on the bias for a graceful drape. Topped with a coordinating wrap in deep lilac, Francesca would look lovely. No frills, no flounces, no unnecessary material to detract from her natural loveliness.

Giselle doodled on the next blank page and considered earth mothers like Chelsea. Giselle knew that women like Chelsea just wanted comfort, comfort, and more comfort after a full day nurturing everyone and everything other than themselves. What could be more comfortable than an oversized Sleep Tee in prewashed, American-grown cotton? Depending on the season, the Tee would be available with cap sleeves for warmer weather, and long sleeves with picot trim for winter. A pale leaf pattern on a background of wheat, soft sage, or forest green would be just right, no matter the season.

The Hillary's of the world were definitely a challenge, even for the most experienced designers. Giselle wanted to create something that would conceal the sharp angles on their thin frames while making them feel good inside. Perhaps a line of full-length, plush chenille robes—with shawl collars, deep pockets, turn-back cuffs, and some new, oversized buttons. Giselle didn't want to add any sashes that would accentuate the waist. She wanted these robes to feel like big, warm bear hugs. As for colors, the robes should be available in only gentle colors of baby blue, rose pink, light lemon and tender peach.

Sarah…Mmm…How would one describe Sarah? Giselle closed her eyes and let the words come into her mind—Sincere…Sensitive…Stressed… Giselle had always wanted to design an entire collection of spa wear for women who needed a day (or two or three) away. Giselle sketched out an above-the-knee length kimono in soothing colors of pale-pink raspberry and cloud blue. Women like Sarah could pack the kimono in an overnight bag and take off for a relaxing, well-deserved weekend of pampering at *The*

Spa at Norwich Inn. A terry sarong with shirred top would be perfect, too, and would also pack well. Now that she thought about it, maybe she should suggest that the Bronxville Book Club hold one of their meetings at a spa. Lizbet would be absolutely thrilled to organize all the details.

And last but not least, Madison…the Book Club's very own money honey. Traditional button-front silk pajamas with ¾ length sleeves and a relaxed drawstring bottom with elastic waist would suit Madison and her colleagues quite well after a hard day of work in Manhattan. For warmer evenings, Madison could cover the pj's with a loosely belted, deliciously luxurious cashmere robe. Color? The color of money, of course.

For herself, Giselle would design something very, very special. She uncrossed her legs and walked over to the rosewood bookshelves. Scanning the top shelf, she pulled out several dusty Barbara Cartland paperbacks for inspiration. Sitting back down, Giselle smiled and began to draw. She knew just what Massimo would like.

"Never go to a doctor
whose office plants have died."

Erma Bombeck

Chapter 19

Chelsea

greenthum@graciousgardens.com

Chelsea hit the remote-controlled door opener and swung her Jeep into the garage. She gingerly opened the car door, carefully maneuvered around all the gardening equipment, and then activated the door close panel.

For years Chelsea and Ted had been talking about renovating their outdated garage, or "original carriage house" as the realtor described it when she sold them the house. Yes, the carriage house was absolutely charming, but it had been built long before automobiles made their appearance. With Ted's lovingly restored 1955 T-Bird convertible, her Jeep, and a Volkswagen Jetta they were holding onto—since Michael would be getting his learner's permit in the frighteningly near future—as well as several mountain bikes and garden tools, they knew they needed more options than they had with their current setup.

Ted had talked to the contractor their neighbors Will and Georgia Lawford had used. The Lawfords had just finished constructing a custom-designed heated "garage" with ceramic tile floor and built-in cabinetry. Chelsea wouldn't want anything nearly as grand. She remembered reading an article a few years ago in the *New York Times* that noted that several "Garage Mahals" had been built in Bronxville. Chelsea had been hired for a similar project in Scarsdale in which a new terrace had been erected over the family's expanded three-car garage. Will had estimated that it would cost Chelsea and Ted about $150,000-$200,000 to design and construct their own garage and terrace at current costs—and that took into account that Chelsea would do her own landscaping!

Chelsea and Tom were doing well financially and could probably afford it, but both felt very strongly that they wanted to maintain the architectural integrity and character of the original structure. They would not make the same mistakes that Anne and Donald were making. They knew a renovation could be done in such a way that a new addition would integrate well with the existing house. The proof that it could be done right was in that exquisite house on Oriole where the owners had just completed a major renovation. The new sand-colored stucco garage gracefully blended with the existing house and incorporated a magnificent new terrace and screened in gazebo. Chelsea could just see herself sitting in the gazebo surrounded by her favorite flowers, sipping Cranberry herb tea while reading a good book.

She could dream. But for now, they would work with what they had.

Turning away from the garage, Chelsea noticed her calico cat, Gracie, sitting in the chaise lounge that the kids had given her last Mother's Day. Chelsea accepted Gracie's silent invitation, and joined her on the chair. As she massaged the soft fur under Gracie's chin, she surveyed her yard, wondering if it was true that the shoemaker's children had no shoes. She was a landscape architect, but if she was honest with herself, she would admit that her yard was a bit neglected. One more thing to add to the endless list. She told herself it was a good thing that she didn't have that new gazebo and terrace yet—she would need time to take care of it, something that was in very short supply these days.

The kids were still teasing her about the green notice from the Village of Bronxville Department of Public Works that had been stuffed in their mailbox last week.

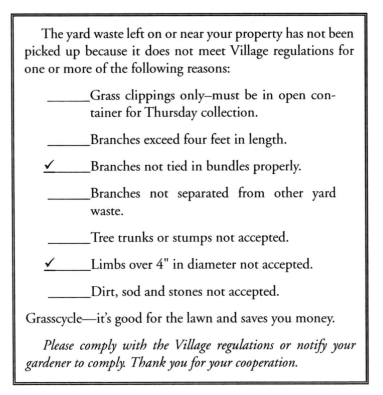

The yard waste left on or near your property has not been picked up because it does not meet Village regulations for one or more of the following reasons:

_____Grass clippings only–must be in open container for Thursday collection.

_____Branches exceed four feet in length.

✓_____Branches not tied in bundles properly.

_____Branches not separated from other yard waste.

_____Tree trunks or stumps not accepted.

✓_____Limbs over 4" in diameter not accepted.

_____Dirt, sod and stones not accepted.

Grasscycle—it's good for the lawn and saves you money.

Please comply with the Village regulations or notify your gardener to comply. Thank you for your cooperation.

When she had a spare moment, Chelsea would have to speak with herself about her noncompliance.

How on earth did the Kate Reddy's of the world do it? Chelsea wished she had read the book. Maybe she would have picked up some tips on "having it all" or at least enjoyed a good laugh at the expense of those who still believed it was possible to have it all.

Certainly Kathryn didn't have it all. Chelsea could remember when she used to handle all of Kathryn and David's landscaping needs. The twice-weekly lawn service had been one of the first things to go after the divorce. But maybe Kathryn had a latent gardening gene because her property still looked well tended. Although judging by her manicure, Kathryn certainly wasn't out there pulling any weeds herself.

Lizbet still asked Chelsea for advice about her garden, but at this point Lizbet's plants and trees were very mature; the perennials were doing splendidly and didn't need to be replaced any time soon. (If Chelsea allowed herself a catty thought, maybe the gardens were more mature than Lizbet.) But Lizbet could be loads of fun. Just last week Chelsea and Lizbet had attended the Central Park Conservancy awards luncheon to raise money for the park. Lizbet's dramatic, wide-brimmed, linen dress hat, decorated with berry pink roses and seed pearls, was gorgeous…and of course she wore it as only she could.

Much to her dismay, Carole didn't have any kids of her own in the school, or any property to landscape, so she and Chelsea didn't have much in common. They had never discussed Algebra or Azaleas. But even if they had something in common, Chelsea just did not get good vibes about the woman—she oozed bitterness from every pore.

Chelsea didn't know Hillary all that well either, but her garden was picture perfect and looked like something out of *Better Homes & Gardens*. Chelsea wasn't sure which landscaper Bradford and Hillary used, but the color and variety of the perennials that were planted was quite unusual for this area. Chelsea wasn't jealous, though. There certainly was enough business in Bronxville for several landscape architects, and Chelsea barely had time to take care of the clients she already had.

While her property wasn't large, Francesca did such a terrific job with the plants and flowers she cultivated on her terrace at Bolton Gardens. Chelsea should remember to drop off some new plants for her when she got in the next shipment. Francesca seemed like such a nice person, and Chelsea needed to make more of an effort to get to know her better. Chelsea was still smiling about Francesca's unexpected performance at the meeting tonight. She really brought the book to life! One could only imagine what other talents she might be hiding. Michael was taking French next year, but maybe Chelsea should encourage Lucas to consider taking Spanish in Middle School. From what Chelsea observed, Francesca had all the makings of a great teacher.

Chelsea still considered Madison to be her #1 favorite customer. She first met Madison when they worked on the Strategic Planning Committee at the school. Fortunately for Chelsea, Madison was in need of a new landscape architect. Based on her good friend Sarah's recommendation,

Madison hired Chelsea on the spot. Madison had always been so agreeable to Chelsea's suggestions for her property, and was only too happy to delegate the responsibility for all the landscaping decisions to Chelsea. If only all her clients were so agreeable and had such confidence in her ability!

Anne had approached Chelsea about becoming a client, but Chelsea would not get involved in the landscaping for the McMansion, no matter what the Richardsons were willing to pay. Not only did she object to it on principle, but also her other clients in town would absolutely disown her. Chelsea vowed to stay as far away from that political hot potato as possible.

Thinking about Anne reminded Chelsea to give Dorothy Brennan a call. Dorothy would have the latest scoop on the proposed legislation to ban the leveling of prominent village trees. It was a shame you couldn't rely on all residents to exercise good judgement and demonstrate community responsibility. As Ted often said—and Anne and Donald proved—some people have more money than sense.

Chelsea heard the TV coming from the open window in the upstairs bedroom. She knew she should get up and head inside, maybe even finish that landscaping proposal for the corner property on Summit, but it was so peaceful out here in the garden. She closed her eyes and leaned back in the chaise. She tried not to think about all that she had to do. Instead, she thought, "Maybe this year I'll get my House Elf for Christmas." Chelsea repeated a phrase from one of her favorite movies. "I believe…I believe…I believe." If it worked for little Virginia in *Miracle on 34th Street*, it could work for Chelsea. She believed!

"When angry, count to four;
when very angry, swear."

Pudd'nhead Wilson's Calendar

Chapter 20

Carole

christmascarole@eventplanning.org

arole found a parking spot on Sagamore Road and locked her Toyota. On nights like this, after spending an evening at such an unbelievably gorgeous home—so close and yet so far—Carole felt especially resentful of Alexandra...and her living in what should have been *Carole* and Andrew's home on Sunset and Paradise.

Carole walked quickly to her apartment building and flung open the downstairs door much harder than she had intended. She stopped by the row of mailboxes in the lobby to compose herself. Carole felt herself getting worked up all over again and resolved to put Alexandra out of her mind so she could salvage what was left of the evening. With great effort, she banished all thoughts of Alexandra (or most anyway) and climbed the stairs of her fourth-floor walk-up.

All was peacefully quiet as Carole paused on the landing before entering the apartment. Hopefully the girls were in the second bedroom doing their homework, so that she and Andrew could make up and spend some quality private-time alone. Maybe the day wouldn't be a total loss. With some scented candles, soft music, a little wine, perhaps tonight they could reasonably discuss Carole's desire for a baby.

Unlocking the door, Carole stepped into the foyer and dropped her keys and purse on the small table next to the hall closet. Before she went into the bedroom to see Andrew, she needed to review her plans for Friday so that she could have a clear head. She reached into the wicker basket underneath the table and pulled out her bulky "To Do" folder. Since

Carole had to give up her second bedroom when the girls stayed over, she was forced to find some creative places to keep her important papers accessible at all times.

Nothing in her life was easy. Her fundraising projects required more of her attention than ever before. With investment banking bonuses decreasing, and Westchester property taxes increasing—largely to pay for those sacrosanct medical and pension benefits of civil service employees—the Arts Council was competing for the same shrinking pool of donations as many other sister organizations.

Scanning the neatly typed pages of items that needed her attention, Carole prioritized the list and focused on the top four.

❧ TO DO ❧

1. Call Rachel at the *Westchester Wag*. Tell Rachel that the announcement about the Family Services of Westchester golf outing will be e-mailed to her no later than Friday afternoon. It must be included in their "Registry of Galas and Benefits" column in the next issue. Timing is critical!

Event:	*Family Services of Westchester's Sixth Annual Golf Outing*
Date:	*June 28*
Location:	*Winged Foot Golf Club*
Description:	*Annual golf outing offers both morning and afternoon shotguns at this highly distinguished golf club. Includes golf caddy, breakfast, lunch, and dinner, and awards reception.*
Chairperson:	*J. Parker Atkinson*
Ticket Price:	*$625 per golfer; $2400 for a foursome*
Contact:	*Carole Collins christmascarole@eventplanning.org*

☞ TO DO ☜

2.   Call Spencer Hartman to get names of gourmet chefs/local businesses that participated in the Jansen Memorial Hospice's "Better Than Cooking" Benefit Reception at the Field Club.

      Follow-up with calls to each of the businesses to discuss sponsorship of Westchester Arts Council programs.

3.   Set up lunch with Jill and Diana at the Mamaroneck Beach and Yacht Club to review menu, flowers, music, photography, journal, décor and invitations for the Special Olympics fundraiser.

      Get Diana and Jill's input on suggested names to Chair the event—Mary Civillo? Joan Lunden? Meredith Vieira?

4.   Call Karen to see if the Blue Hill Troupe is available to perform at the gala concert to benefit Lawrence Hospital scheduled for October 20.

      Back-up plan:
      Call Clyde to see if the University Glee Club of New York City has the date free.

With her plans for tomorrow in place, Carole felt she could concentrate on relaxing with Andrew for the rest of the evening. She just wanted to see him and put this awful day behind them. She quietly moved down the narrow hallway so as not to disturb the girls—actually so that they wouldn't disturb her—and listened at their door. Carole could hear Courtney and Mackenzie talking, but not to each other. They were probably on their cell phones.

Carole continued down the corridor and opened the door to their crowded bedroom. Andrew was absently thumbing through *Entertainment Weekly* and sipping a Corona. The portable TV on the triple dresser was tuned to CNN, but the volume was almost inaudible. Andrew looked a little distracted as she approached and gave him a quick kiss on the check. He zapped Larry King with the remote and sighed as Carole asked about his evening. He explained that he had just finished a long conference call with his branch office in California. One of the junior attorneys had heard through the grapevine that some of the kids from the latest reality shows were looking for legal advice. Andrew knew they needed a whole team of lawyers just to help them sort through all the contracts that were being thrown at them. It was unbelievable. They were getting offers that spanned everything from putting **on** clothes with the *Old Navy* logo, to taking **off** clothes for *Playboy*. Andrew was pushing to get a meeting set up with these kids before their fifteen minutes of fame were up.

Carole tried to make her voice sound light as she asked about Alexandra.

"No, Carole, I haven't talked to Alexandra. She must have her cell phone off."

"Andrew, don't you hate it when she calls at the last minute, and…"

"Yes, Carole, I hate it when she pulls these stunts, but it isn't the girls' fault, and we need to be careful not to take it out on them."

Carole took a deep breath and tried again. "Are they still studying?"

"Yes, they're in the other room finishing their homework. They've been very quiet."

"Drew, did you remember to…"

"Yes, dear, I remembered to check Mackenzie's math. Carole, you are beginning to sound like Alexandra. Could you please give me a break?" And that was all it took. Carole snapped.

She heard Andrew throw the magazine against the wall as she stormed out of the room and went into the L-shaped living/dining area. Angrily she tossed aside the seat cushions and yanked out the Castro Convertible. She grabbed some clean sheets and a lightweight blanket from the linen closet and quickly made up the couch bed. She climbed onto the uncomfortable mattress, jerked the covers up to her neck, and quietly seethed.

Conjuring up her yoga instructor's voice, Carole closed her emerald-green eyes and began a series of deep-breathing exercises to calm down.

Some fairy tale.

This was definitely not looking good for her plans to have a baby and live happily ever after.

"One of the symptoms of an approaching nervous breakdown is the belief that one's work is terribly important."

Bertrand Russell

Chapter 21

Sarah

inhumanresource@womeninbanking.com

I t was so kind of Kathryn to drive Madison and Sarah home, even though they lived only a few streets over on The Byway. Neither of them had been in any condition to drive. Now Sarah would have to get up extra early to retrieve her husband Roger's Porsche that she had driven to the meeting.

Sarah wondered why on earth she had consumed so much wine on an empty stomach? Her head was still pounding. Moving ever so slowly around the kitchen, she made a fresh pot of Starbuck's Arabian Mocha Java and sat down at the oak table in the breakfast nook off the kitchen. It had been two hours since she had been dropped off at her door, and the caffeine was just beginning to kick in. As Sarah sipped her coffee, she skimmed the label on the coffee package. Here eyes widened. No wonder she liked it so much. The Java beans were blended with wine-like Arabian mocha coffee.

If she was honest with herself, tonight had been Sarah's wake up call. The drinking had to stop. This was not like her. She stood up and grabbed Sundance's leash from the hook by the back door as he looked up at her expectantly. "C'mon Sundance, we both could use a good walk."

The night air felt good and helped Sarah to think. She knew she needed to make some major changes in her life. Particularly since 9/11, Sarah had been trying with renewed determination to focus on what was truly important to her. She had lost a close friend who had been working on the 97th floor of the North Tower that sunny Tuesday morning in September when the first plane hit the World Trade Center. Sarah didn't need a more chilling reminder that as Roger always said, "Life is not a dress rehearsal." It was time to get her life back on track.

Although her brain was certainly still clouded by the alcohol, one thing was crystal clear to Sarah. A decision she had been struggling with for months suddenly seemed so easy. She and Roger had talked about it on numerous occasions, and he had assured her he would support whatever decision she reached. Now Sarah was sure. She would "retire" like her friend Samantha.

Sam was Sarah's role model. After a phenomenally successful career as a senior marketing executive for L'Oreal, she cashed in her stock options, tendered her resignation, and retired at the ripe old age of 46. Sam had been there, done that, and wasn't going to do it anymore. It had been over two years since she had bid adieu to L'Oreal, and Sam still insisted she had no regrets. (Well, perhaps there was one small regret—it was awfully hard to give up those deeply discounted beauty supplies she got at the Company Store.) Maybe Sarah would finally follow Sam's lead as she had been encouraging her to do. Sam often asked, "If you don't have to, why do you want to continue as an ax woman for JP Morgan Chase Citi Bank of America, or whatever the bank will someday be called if you had to live through one more merger?" Sarah could no longer think of a single reason to continue.

Roger had made it clear they would do just fine without Sarah's salary if she wanted to quit. They might have to cut back a little, but not so much that it would impact their day-to-day lives. They would deal with the inevitable changes that it would bring. Roger didn't want to unduly influence Sarah, but he had hinted how nice it would be to come home and have a real family dinner together before it was too late.

Their daughter Ruthann would be heading off to Georgetown in the fall, and with Dylan starting at the High School next year, he wasn't far behind. What kind of role model was Sarah being for her children? Was this the kind of future she would want Ruthann or Dylan to have? She had always told her children things like, "Find your passion…Work is too important to be play, but you should have fun…If your mountain has a summit, you've climbed the wrong mountain…Make sure to have balance in your life." Well, Sarah's passion for the job was a memory, she hadn't laughed at work in ages; she wanted to get off the mountain she was standing on and climb new mountains; and she sorely needed to recapture some of the balance that was missing in her life.

Sarah hoped the rumors about another 15% across-the-board layoff were true. As an HR professional, she knew how the system worked. She would find a way to make it known to the powers that be that she wouldn't mind being in that 15% group this time. She would find out more tomorrow when she attended the strategy meeting in Jersey City where the Bank was planning to expand their new operations center. Her boss Carter should be there as well, and she would schedule some time to talk with him.

Carter was actually one of the more understanding executives she worked with; he and Sarah had been colleagues for years and had survived many a merger and reorganization together. They had first met when they both worked at the Irving Trust Company at One Wall Street. After Irving's merger with the Bank of New York, Carter went to JP Morgan while Sarah ended up at Chase. Chase, which had previously merged with the newly-reorganized Chemical—which had recently emerged from its union with Manny Hanny—had subsequently merged with JP Morgan, so now Sarah and Carter both worked for the new JP Morgan Chase. Carter and she often joked that soon JP Morgan Chase would merge with Bank of New York and call the new bank the Irving Trust Company, thereby bringing them full circle.

Carter also lived in Westchester, in what used to be the quiet hamlet of Chappaqua; that is, before the Clintons and their entourage moved in, and there went the neighborhood! Carter understood all too well why Sarah dreaded the twice-weekly commute to the Jersey City location. It was difficult enough to reach that site before 9/11, when the bank had just a small back-office operation housed there. Back then it had taken her *only* an hour-and-a-half to get there. Since 9/11, so many companies had relocated large groups of employees to the now-popular location just across the Hudson River. All those people traveling to the newly-erected office buildings had to navigate congested PATH stations that had never been designed for the human wave that flowed through the turnstiles each day. Nowadays, it took Sarah an average of two hours from the time she left her home in Westchester until she reached that office. The New York Waterway ferry was an option, but getting across midtown Manhattan to the pier at 38th St and 12th Avenue was a hassle, and the ferries ran only every half hour. Sarah invariably arrived at the pier one minute after the ferry had pushed away from the dock.

Madison also had encouraged Sarah to think seriously about life after JP Morgan Chase. Madison wasn't even remotely thinking about slowing down her own hectic schedule, but she could sense how burned out Sarah had become, and she thought Sarah needed to at least consider some other options. Sarah hated to admit it, but she was scared. For the past twenty years, she had operated within a rigid corporate structure that stifled every last shred of creativity. She just didn't know what she would do if she "retired" and left the corporate womb. But as Oprah's good friend Dr. Phil might say, "If you did know, what would it be?"

Sarah actually did have a few ideas. As she and Sundance rounded the corner of The High Road, she reviewed her wish list of what she might like to do if she had the time and opportunity. It was easy to come up with the very first item on her list—she wanted to work with children.

Sarah had always wanted to devote more time to her volunteer activities at *Heartsong, Inc.*, a wonderful organization that provided music and art therapy for children with disabilities. Whenever she helped out, she was convinced that she got much more out of it than the children did.

Switching Sundance's leash to her left hand, Sarah rooted around in her jacket pocket with her right. No luck. She wished she had a pen and any scrap of paper to jot down some of the other things she would like to do. Somehow seeing it on paper would make it more real for her. Sarah tried to memorize the thoughts as they came into her head. She visualized a neatly typed list with bullet points of the things she had dreamed about over the years.

- Train for the NYC marathon.

- Organize Dylan and Ruthann's baby pictures.

- Go to *Stop & Stop* at off peak hours.

- Throw her Blackberry in the garbage disposal.

- Read a book from cover to cover—perhaps one of the novels the book club had "discussed" over the years.

- Write a book. (Hadn't she and her colleagues joked for years that they could write a book. She remembered that officer they had discovered getting busy with his assistant in the safe deposit box booth. You couldn't make that stuff up!)

- Spend more time with her mother.

- Take a cooking, or gardening, or literature, or music appreciation course. Why not take all of them? There was so much she wanted to learn.

- Teach a course. (Business Communications? Sarah certainly had perfected that skill over the last 20 years.)

- Invent something useful. How about a pill to give to men so they would recognize that objects at the bottom of the stairs needed to be carried to the next floor?

- Take a Cruise to Nowhere with Roger and just enjoy the journey.

- Throw out all the pizza and Chinese food take-out menus.

- Be at home for those exasperating repairmen that had a problem with commitment—the ones who would be there sometime between the hours of 1 and 4 on a Tuesday.

- Travel for fun, not business, and actually see something in another country besides the inside of the conference center.

- Learn how to grow a variety of roses and then stop to smell them.

The possibilities were limitless.

"Sooner or later we all quote our mothers."

Bern Williams

Chapter 22

Madison

munnyhunny@jaegerwood.com

adison crawled up the stairs to her bedroom without turning on a single light. Her head was throbbing and she could barely tolerate even the dimmest light. She made it into the bathroom, splashed some cold water on her face, and moved in slow motion down the hall to Cole's room.

Thank God Cole's stereo was not on. When she knocked softly on his door, Cole smiled a hello. He was multitasking, as usual. Madison thought she was good at juggling, but wondered how Cole could be on his laptop revising a Word document, instant messaging his friends, watching MTV, and talking on his cell phone to his girlfriend, Molly. Ah youth! She waved, blew a kiss, and quietly closed his door.

Madison would miss her son so much when he left home for college in a year, but she knew it was his time and she and John were happy for him. Cole had been a fairly easy child and hadn't given her and John too many sleepless nights. His grades were consistently good, and his teachers always remarked what a pleasure he was to have in class. Cole's circle of friends was small, but they were close and looked out for each other. He had known many of them since kindergarten, and had gotten into some innocent mischief with a few. Madison could have done without some of the things Cole had done over the years—like the Halloween egg fight on the Hilltop; or when he "borrowed" John's new Lexus (busted by the EZ Pass statement); or the time he hosted an impromptu sophomore pool party when she was away visiting her sister. But all things considered, Cole's teenage years hadn't been too bad so far.

Looking back, Madison was glad that they had not enrolled Cole in the Choate Rosemary Hall boarding school, as they had originally planned for him upon his completion of the Middle School. Close friends were absolutely appalled that John and Madison were even considering it. "With all the school taxes you pay, you're going to send your only child to prep school?" Even closer friends had added, "Are you nuts?!!!" Madison herself had been conflicted. She had always felt that School Board members who sent their own children to private schools didn't exactly inspire confidence. Thankfully, John and she saw eye-to-eye on this one. Cole stayed at Bronxville.

Madison knew how fortunate they were that Cole wasn't one of the teenagers whose beer cans littered Chambers football field after a Saturday night celebrating a Bronco's team victory. One Sunday morning, while she walked the track with Sarah, Madison had been embarrassed for a petite teen-aged girl who came down to the field to retrieve a Kate Spade bag she had apparently lost during the festivities the night before. Cole hadn't joined in such "festivities" yet, but he still had to get through senior year, so John and Madison were definitely not complacent.

In a recent article in the Westchester section of the *Sunday Times*, Madison had read yet another editorial on teenage drinking in which the Superintendent of the Bronxville Schools had been quoted. She agreed with Dr. Gemmill that, "The patterns of alcohol usage cut across economic lines, but they get reported on in the highly visible communities." Well, they certainly lived in that kind of community! Lots of villages and towns had problems with alcohol, especially at the senior proms, but a few years back, when some of the Bronxville students had misbehaved *so* badly that the faculty and administration cancelled the prom, it made the national news.

John and Madison weren't quite sure what the secret of their childrearing success was—after all, they knew wonderful people in the town whose children were doing some not so wonderful things. Even before Cole was born, Madison had begun reading all the latest theories about bringing up baby.

She really liked one book that had an entire chapter on catching a child doing something right and rewarding the positive behavior. She knew she had made mistakes with Cole—not her finest moment in the *Food Emporium* when she had screamed at him for dropping the eggs he was loading into the cart—but she tried her best.

As Cole entered Middle School, Madison attended numerous evening workshops sponsored by the PTA. She especially remembered one of the speakers at the Family University program who reminded the parents that teenagers needed to be protected from their own impulses. He advised them not to sweat the small stuff—like burgundy hair, messy rooms, or temporary tattoos of Britney. Like Britney, the tattoos would be forgotten soon enough. The speaker also underscored that both parents needed to be clear about the consequences for unacceptable behaviors, and then follow-through. Madison's mother must have been ahead of her time—she definitely believed in following through on her threats. It scared Madison, but she could hear her mother saying, "Someday you'll thank me for this." Although Madison would never admit it to her face, her mother was actually right! It was funny how once Cole knew that both she and John were prepared to follow through with the "punishment", even if it also meant punishing themselves, the bad behavior generally disappeared.

With all the challenges and tough assignments she had faced throughout her life, Madison felt that being a parent was absolutely the most difficult job on earth. No contest. She felt that parenting was more than a full-time job, and she took it very seriously.

Never one to take *any* of her responsibilities lightly, Madison knew she should review the latest Board package for next week's meeting. But she also knew that she wasn't in the right frame of mind to wade through the latest updates on the construction project—maybe they should encourage Cole to become a bricklayer or carpenter?—or prepare for the strategic plan meeting with the High School Principal. While being a mother might be the first most difficult job on earth, Madison would argue that being Principal of the Bronxville High School was a close second. She remembered when a previous Administrator had commented that Bronxville had a history of eating their High School Principals for breakfast. The

Elementary School might have the Muffia, but the High School definitely had what she had come to call the **Fuffia.**

Fathers of

Unbelievably

Frenzied

Future

Ivy League

Applicants

If Kate Reddy thought the Muffia was a force to be reckoned with, wait until her little ones reached High School where the stakes got exponentially higher. Using skills honed in mahogany-paneled boardrooms across Manhattan, the Fuffia began to appear at school meetings and evening coffees and make their powerful presence known. They didn't raise their voices or mince words. It was quite clear that for their progeny, nothing less than a smooth passage into their ivy-covered alma maters would be acceptable. Madison could easily visualize a member of the Fuffia in his corner office suite overlooking Park Avenue, Montblanc pen poised to write the first tuition check to Harvard for young W. Hartwick Hamilton Hedgeworth IV.

*Muffia…Fuffia…*Just thinking about them made Madison feel even more tired. She contemplated checking her Blackberry but thought better of it. One night of being unplugged would not bring the firm of Jaeger, Wood & Fenwick to its knees. Tomorrow would be soon enough to deal with the inevitable e-mails, voice mails, and FedEx packages that would be waiting in her office at 7:30 a.m.

Feeling insatiably thirsty, Madison dragged herself down to the kitchen for a Diet Snapple Iced Tea. Using her dwindling strength to twist off the cap, she took a long drink. Before consigning the empty bottle to the recycling bin, she looked inside the cap and read Snapple's Real Fact" #55. "A human brain weighs around 3 pounds." Hopefully no one would mention that fact to Hillary—there was no telling what she might do to lose those pesky extra 3 pounds.

How was she ever going to get up at 5:45 a.m. tomorrow? Holding onto the balustrade, Madison pulled herself back up the stairs to her bedroom to lay out her clothes for the morning. John had fallen asleep with the television on again. She covered him up and turned off his reading light. Maybe it was the wine that caused her to gaze a little longer at her husband and reflect on their years together. John was a bit grayer and a bit thicker around the middle, but Madison was happy she had married him twenty years ago. Cole would do just fine to follow in John's footsteps, even if he was a charter member of the Fuffia.

Madison picked up the remote control and flipped through the channels until she hit Channel 74. Even in her slightly tipsy condition she was horrified to see herself on the rebroadcast of the last School Board meeting. She sounded halfway intelligent, but could not one of her friends have told her that she looked like a skunk? She reached for her Palm Pilot on the night table and made a note to call *Studio One*—she absolutely had to get her roots retouched before the next meeting.

She turned off the TV, but Madison was still wired. Maybe she would read a bit before bed. She just wished she remembered what they had agreed on for the book selection for next month. Wait a minute…Did they even pick a book?

Thank goodness Lizbet would remember. What would they ever do without her?

"If you want to know what God thinks of money, just look at the people he gave it to."

Dorothy Parker

Chapter 23

Lizbet

whippenpoof@thebronxvillebookclub.com

izbet pulled out her Tiffany key ring and unlocked her front door. She stepped into the family room and checked the messages on the machine and on the heart-shaped pad by the phone. There were nine phone calls to return, which was not too bad, considering Memorial Day was next week.

Deb had called at 8:00 to find out about the tents for the Festival-on-the-Green. It seems the custodial staff had moved them for safekeeping after last year's rain, and now the tents were missing. With all the confusion surrounding the construction, Lizbet thought it was no wonder the staff couldn't find them. Lizbet would have to go down to the school tomorrow and check it out herself.

The second message was from Nan, just confirming that they were meeting for coffee tomorrow morning. Unless she heard from Lizbet beforehand, Nan said she would be at *Slave to the Grind* at the usual time. Val, Kelly, and Peggy would definitely be there too. Hunter had a yoga class, but she would come over as soon as it ended.

Lizbet was very disappointed after playing back Olivia's voicemail. "Hi, Lizbet. I can't make tennis tomorrow at 10:30. Tom and I decided to take *NetJets* to the Vineyard, and we won't be back until late Monday night. Will Tuesday work for you?" Lizbet didn't want to cancel her tennis match. She was counting on wearing her new tennis dress, in the requisite club white, with just the thinnest band of cobalt blue on the collar. She decided that maybe she'd wear it anyway when she met her friends for coffee.

The fourth message was from Marikay to reassure Lizbet that the Pepsi products her company was donating would be delivered as scheduled. Also, Marikay's friend in Marketing had come across a cache of water bottles, and if Lizbet wanted to use them as prizes for the games, she was more than welcome to take all of them.

Addison Anderson, Junior Class President, had checked in to see if Lizbet had a final count of the number of basketballs and hoops they would have available for the jump-shot contest. He had plenty of volunteers, so the more equipment she had, the more kids they could handle.

Tania's phone call was next. "Lizbet, stop worrying. The trophies for the *Run for Fun* have arrived at last. They are even nicer than the ones we gave out last year. You will be so pleased." Tania went on to say that she was putting together a foursome for golf on Wednesday and would love it if Lizbet were available to play. Lizbet thought she was free that day, but she wondered who else was being asked to round out the foursome. She made a note to find out who else would be there before making any definite commitment.

Renee's voice on the answering machine sounded stressed. "Lizbet, I need your help, ASAP! There's a problem with the rock-climbing wall, something about the insurance. I don't know what to do, and the insurance company keeps calling me for more information. If I don't get back to them by tomorrow afternoon, they say they won't give us the required permit." Lizbet would call the school's insurance carrier first thing in the morning. It just would not be acceptable to cancel this new attraction. It was guaranteed to be a hit.

Whitney's English tutor, Meg, was playing telephone tag with Lizbet. "Hi, this is Meg. I got your message. I can fit Whitney in for two extra sessions each week if that's what you want. Just get back to me by tomorrow evening; my open slots are filling up fast." Lizbet jotted a note to call Meg *first* thing in the morning. The problem with the rock-climbing wall would just have to wait.

The last call was from Barbara about the raffle. "Lizbet, do you have any more ticket books? My committee needs more, more, more! Kudos to whoever came up with the brilliant idea of *Beauty for the Beast*. The grand prize of a day of grooming, followed by a formal studio portrait of the family pet, really is helping to sell a lot of tickets!"

Lizbet would be disappointed when Memorial Day was over. Planning the event had entailed so much work, but it also had been so much fun. Lizbet would miss all the meetings, phone calls, lunches, and coffees that were part and parcel of such a huge undertaking. However, with Whitney being a senior next year, there were probably a hundred other activities and committees that could use Lizbet's talents. Maybe she would volunteer to organize the traditional High School Graduation ceremony held on the front lawn. It was such an elegant ceremony, unique to Bronxville—the girls wore gorgeous white ball gowns from the *House of Boticelli*, and carried large bouquets of long-stemmed, red roses; the boys were handsomely dressed in white dinner jackets, with red rose boutonnières. Lizbet also could plan the gently used white dress sale for seniors...and the parent appreciation dinner...and the baccalaureate ceremony. She should really get started putting together some new committees so that it would be her, she meant *Whitney's*, best senior year ever.

Brimming with ideas, Lizbet went upstairs and knocked on Whitney's door. "How was Taylor's? Did you come up with a lot of wonderful ideas for the Yearbook?" Lizbet didn't mind that Whitney and Taylor were both vying for the plum position of Yearbook Editor since this year two seniors would be selected to serve as Co-Editors. Whitney was obviously much more qualified than Taylor was, but as long as Whitney was selected as one of the Co-Editors, Lizbet wasn't concerned. Lizbet would have to talk to the consultant who was writing Whitney's college application. Why even mention the "Co" part of Editor when he showcased Whitney's accomplishments?

Lizbet said goodnight to her daughter and walked towards the master bedroom suite at the end of the hall. Grant was still awake reading in their antique sleigh bed. Lizbet sat down on the champagne silk chaise lounge and slipped off her sandals, admiring her pedicure. Grant glanced up from his Tom Clancy novel and inquired about her day.

"Well, Grant, it has been such a long day, but quite satisfying."

"Did Lucy pick up my suits from *Spic and Span* before she ran those errands you left for her?"

"Yes, didn't you see them? When you walk into your closet, they're hanging on the right hand side. She also picked up your dress shirts while she was there."

"What did Lucy do to these sheets?"

"Why, she sprayed them with lavender water when she ironed them. Don't you love it?"

He peered at her over his rimless reading glasses. "Frankly, Lizbet, you need to tell Lucy…"

"Now, Grant, don't start. We have been over this at least a hundred times. You may be the CEO at work, but I am the Chief Executive Officer of this household, and if you think it's so easy…"

"Lizbet, how was the book club meeting?"

Happy to change the subject, Lizbet brightened. "It was a really good meeting actually. About ten of the women showed up tonight, and not surprisingly, since I was one of the few who had actually read the book, I had to lead the discussion."

Oblivious to the fact that Grant had returned to his book, Lizbet continued her recap of the evening. "As you can well imagine, I had to guide the discussion to ensure that the meeting was a success. And, of course, I felt obliged to help poor Kathryn with her hostessing duties. It can't be easy being on her own now, without a husband, and no live-in household help. We really should have Kathryn over for dinner sometime, don't you agree?"

Before Grant could respond to her rhetorical question, Lizbet picked up where she left off. "Speaking of dinner, Anne Richardson was there and tried to trap me into accepting a dinner party invitation, but let's not dwell on that unpleasant woman. We will not be having dinner with her now, or ever. I'd rather be seen dining at McDonalds than at her McMansion."

Lizbet stepped over to the vanity to remove her makeup. As she applied the Sisley Intensive Night Cream she had picked up at *Saks*, she shifted her attention to Memorial Day. She would have to come up with a really special thank-you party for her committee members. She'd better talk to Mrs.

McGrath to get her started planning the menu. The date would be a problem, since many on the committee would soon be leaving for their summer homes, so Lizbet needed to get on their calendars ASAP.

Lizbet loved parties. She was already looking forward to the book club's annual holiday party in December. She had the most fabulous idea to propose as party favors for each member. *The Bookmouse* in town had these marvelous bookplates made by hand for the collector and the small library. Lizbet would volunteer to head up a committee to work with *The Bookmouse's* designer on a bookplate just for The Bronxville Book Club! She couldn't wait to tell the others and see who would want to join her new committee.

But first, she had better plan all the details for the next meeting. Tomorrow, after her coffee group, Lizbet would stop in at the *Womrath Bookshop* and pick out a good book to read in June. Since she didn't have tennis with Olivia, Lizbet knew she would have no trouble e-mailing the meeting announcement to all the members before the weekend. It was important that she send the notice out quickly—she needed to give these women as much of a head start as possible. They just didn't seem to be as organized as she was, nor, for that matter, did they have the same flair for guiding the book discussions. They were right—what would they do without her?

Rising from the chaise lounge, Lizbet headed into her closet to select her outfit for the morning. It was shaping up to be quite a busy day.

"*I don't care to belong to a club that accepts people like me as members.*"

Groucho Marx

Chapter 24

The June Meeting

****

To: *brokerbabe@bxvillerealestate.com,*
munnyhunny@jaegerwood.com,
legalgenius@carruthersassoc.com,
greenthum@graciousgardens.com,
horsewhisperer@equestriansociety.org,
arichardson@annetiques.com,
bronxvillegrad@nyjuniorleague.com,
christmascarole@eventplanning.org,
modelcitizen@thelingerielady.com,
pcdoc@systemsolutions.com,
maestramama@westchesterteachers.edu,
bookworm@literaryreview.com,
inhumanresource@womeninbanking.com,
never2thin@fitness.org

From: *whippenpoof@thebronxvillebookclub.com*

Subject: *Bronxville Book Club Meeting*

Date: *June 12*

Time: *7:30 p.m.*

Place: *Lizbet Wellington Smith's home*
927 Elm Rock Road

Book: *The Crimson Petal and the White by Michel Faber*

Hope to see you all at our last meeting of the season!!!

****

*L*izbet looked over the e-mail invitation for next month's meeting—the book club's last before they took a break for the summer. Before hitting the Send button, however, she moved her cursor to the distribution list and removed *arichardson@annetiques.com*. If anyone noticed, Lizbet could always blame one of those darn computer viruses. And by the time Anne noticed, hopefully it would be June 13!

Mission accomplished, Lizbet swiveled her chair away from the computer monitor and gazed out through the partially-opened pocket doors that overlooked the in-ground swimming pool. Picking up her newly purchased copy of *The Crimson Petal and the White,* she headed to kitchen for a tall glass of Mrs. McGrath's specially brewed iced tea before heading outside. Selecting a shady spot near the budding red and white impatiens that lined the far end of the deck, Lizbet settled into a generously cushioned lounge chair and turned to the first chapter. She had spent a lot of time researching this book. (After last month's meeting, there was no way she was going to let anyone else choose the book ever again!) Although the hardcover edition was 848 pages, Lizbet knew that, unlike the others, *she* would have no trouble finishing it before the meeting.

This novel sounded very intriguing—a sprawling Victorian era epic about a nineteen-year-old London prostitute named Sugar. From what Lizbet gathered, the well-read, ambitious prostitute gets involved with the son of a wealthy perfumer who lifts her out of the squalor and sets her up in a beautiful house in a fashionable part of London. Lizbet could hardly imagine the distasteful things someone like Sugar would have to do to maintain the lifestyle to which she would grow accustomed. Even though it was so removed from her life in Bronxville, Lizbet thought it sounded like a delightful escape.

"*After the game, the king and the pawn go into the same box.*"

Italian Proverb

Epilogue

~ *September* ~

athryn hurried out of *Mrs. Green's Natural Market* with her arms full and almost collided into Lizbet, who was just turning the corner at Park Place. Kathryn placed both grocery bags on a nearby wooden bench and gave Lizbet a quick hug. "How are you? How was your summer?"

Looking tan and well-rested, Lizbet pushed her Burberry plaid sunglasses atop her head and sighed. "The summer was just too, too short! We missed you. You really should have come out to the beach for a visit!"

Looking considerably less tan and less well-rested, Kathryn silently thought, "You really should have invited me!"

Lizbet bemoaned how crowded all her favorite restaurants and shops had been with all those people who didn't even live in Southampton. Kathryn shook her head in sympathy and politely asked about mutual friends who summered there.

"Jacqueline and Michaela were there, of course. They wanted me to be sure to tell you they send their best. We had to get a new doubles partner since you weren't there to play. Maybe you know her...Abigail Pennington? She has a terrific serve, but her backhand isn't nearly as strong as yours. She rented the Davenport's beach house for July and August while they stayed at their new place in St. Barts. You would not believe how much the rentals were going for this year." Lizbet paused for a moment before deciding that Kathryn would also want to know that she had run into David and his new girlfriend.

"Have you met David's new, um, friend, Brittany? Did Pryce tell you about her?"

Kathryn involuntarily paled. "No, Pryce didn't tell me too much about the weekends he spent with David. He always seemed to have a good time, though." She tried to sound nonchalant. "Did you meet her? What's she like?"

"Grant and I had dinner with them a few times and went sailing with them once. Grant said he thought she was, well, he described her as *perky*."

"Perky? What on earth did he mean by that?"

Lizbet decided—solely out of concern for Pryce—that she should tell Kathryn how appalling it was that David allowed the nineteen-year-old Brittany to sunbathe topless, even if it was on his own boat or in his yard. To Lizbet's utter amazement, Kathryn barely batted an eye at this revelation. She was too busy thinking that Lizbet would have been even more appalled if she knew that Carlo, the new Manny, had been sunbathing topless in Kathryn's backyard those very same weekends!

Kathryn quickly changed the subject.

"Lizbet, your friend Bitsy called me today and asked to see the house on Prescott that you told her was coming on the market…326 Prescott."

"Yes, it would be absolutely perfect for her. Wait until you meet her. You'll just love her. Bitsy, Emma and I all belonged to the same sorority at Yale. Bitsy's planning to move back East, and it will be too much fun having her live in the same town. She is a great reader, so she'll want to join the Book Club, and what a golfer…Grant and I are sponsoring Bitsy and her husband Elliot for Siwanoy membership. We'll all have to play sometime. Emma and I can't wait for her to move in."

"But Lizbet, that house isn't on the market. It belongs to Anne and Donald Richardson."

"Oh, there's Elaine. I really need to talk to her about the High School Graduation committee I'm chairing this year. Gotta run. We'll talk soon. Let's make a date for lunch. My treat!"

Kathryn shook her head and smiled as she retrieved her bags and walked to her Mercedes. She pressed the remote to unlock the trunk and placed the groceries inside. She really should head home, but instead of turning towards Masterton Road, curiosity got the best of her and she drove over to Prescott Avenue.

Anne was just locking her front door as Kathryn pulled into the driveway. She descended the cobblestone steps and walked over to Kathryn's car as she lowered the window.

"Kathryn, what a coincidence. You must be clairvoyant. I was going to call you this evening. I wanted you to be the *first* to know. Donald decided…I mean, Donald and I thought…that is, we both agreed, um…that all things considered…Oh, Kathryn, I might as well cut to the chase. We give up. We're leaving. Donald and I are building a new 7,500 square-foot house in Scarsdale. It will have everything we need, and it's so convenient for me. It's right near one of my other boutiques on Popham Road. So of course that means we need to sell this house. It's just too bad we were never able to finish the renovation. It would have been spectacular. But hopefully there will be a buyer for this old grande dame. Do you think you could handle the marketing of it for us?"

Kathryn stifled a laugh. She wanted to tell Anne, "Don't worry, the Gamma Gamma Girlfriends are way ahead of you. Consider it sold!" Instead, she told Anne she would draw up the contracts as soon as she got back to the office. Kathryn waved goodbye and backed her convertible out of the driveway.

As Kathryn waited at the traffic light, she quickly did the math. She pounded the dashboard and let out a very loud, "Yes!!!" Six-percent commission on that $3,675,000 house was $220,500. Kathryn could afford a live-in again! But this time, it would be so nice to have a Manny around the house.

~ *The End* ~

0-595-28351-9